FIRST PRAYER

Admit Franklin Winters to their meetings! How could they? He was not a Christian. Lois had always liked him very much, but she was afraid he might make fun of what they did.

She had never prayed aloud before in her life, and now to have this young man come—oh! It would be dreadful! It would be an impossibility to pray knowing he was there, listening, judging.

And the help came.

The young man who knelt and listened was amazed. Was this really Lois Peters who was talking in that sweet voice, apparently to some One who stood close beside her and in whom she seemed to have the utmost confidence? And was he being prayed about, too? For the first time in his life, he believed there was something in religion that he did not understand . . . a power that reached into the heart-life as nothing else could do. . . .

THE PARKERSTOWN
DELEGATE
AND OTHER STORIES

Living Books ®
Tyndale House Publishers, Inc.
Wheaton, Illinois

This Tyndale House book
by Grace Livingston Hill
contains the complete text
of the original hardcover edition.
NOT ONE WORD
HAS BEEN OMITTED.

Library of Congress Catalog Card Number 94-60705
ISBN 0-8423-5061-6

Printed in the United States of America

99 98 97 96 95 94
 6   5   4   3   2   1

CONTENTS

The Parkerstown Delegate

THE SHADOWS are long and low on the grass, the sleepy road is muddy, the chestnuts look expectantly down from the laden tree with their eager, prickly faces, all ready to leap when the frost shall give the word, the river glides dreamily along, and the rusty-throated crickets sing and sing the whole day. A busy gray spider works hard to finish certain meshes on the railing of the upper porch. Nothing makes any difference to her any way. She builds her house in a convenient place for catching flies, and when that house fails or breaks she builds another, so on to the end, and then it is all over.

Two men come down the road in blue jeans overalls and checked blouses. One is big, with a large neck and no collar, a sunburned face lengthening into sandy whiskers, a broad, coarse, straw hat and hands in his pockets. The other is younger, with a pleasant face, a manly figure and a spade over his shoulder. They both have large, heavy boots spattered with mud, and walk much with their heels, carrying their feet after them with a sort of a rhythmic curve, shaped something like a tie in music.

"Is Lois coming back soon?" asks the younger of the two men as they near the large white house on the right hand side of the road. There is much hesitation in his manner as he asks the question, but he tries to summon a matter-of-fact tone, and swings his body a little more decidedly.

The large man, however, does not notice, for he suddenly seems to be aroused to a piece of news he has forgotten to impart.

"Well, yes, now you mention it, she is." There is a pleased look in his pale blue eyes and a broad grin of satisfaction over his face as he makes this reply. He is very proud of his daughter Lois, and three months is a long time for her to have been away from home. He wishes all the neighbors to understand that it is a great thing for Lois Peters to be at home once more. "She's coming on this evening's express train, and that's what I'm hurrying home so early for."

There is a glad ring in the young man's voice which he cannot repress as he answers: "Well, I declare! I'm right glad of it. You see Harley's been taking on so of late because she's been gone so long. He says it seems as if she would never come any more."

"You don't say!" says the proud father. "Well, now, that's too bad. I'm glad she's coming. I make no doubt she'll run right over and see him the first thing. How is the little chap these days?"

"Pretty poorly. He doesn't get any better. Some days he's able to be dressed and moved about, but most of the time he has to lie quite still. Mother gets discouraged about him, but the little fellow is as patient as can be. Father says he can't bear to look at him, sometimes, it seems so dreadful to think he can never be well again."

"Yes, it is pretty hard," said the rough man, rubbing his checked sleeve across his eyes; "uncommon hard for the little chap. Well, good-evening! Lois will be right glad to see you over, I have no doubt. She'll come right off to see the little chap, too," and the two men parted, the younger at his father's gate, while the older man passed on down the road toward the village.

"So Lois is coming back again. Well, I'm glad of it," said the young man to himself as he paused a moment by the gate and looked meditatively back up the road he had just come. The distant hills were purpling themselves into their nightcaps, while the sun tore the clouds into scarlet and gold ribbons to adorn them. The young man watched the process a moment as he had watched it many times before, but to-night the gold seemed more glorious than it had for many a sunset eve, and perhaps it was because it reminded him of the light on Lois's face. At least his heart felt that the sunlight of the village was coming back. He had not thought much of it in that way before, it is true; but he was glad, nevertheless, perhaps for his little brother's sake, that Lois was coming back. They had been good friends for years.

There was nothing handsome about Franklin Winters except his great, honest dark eyes, and his smile. People said his smile was like a benediction. That smile lighted up his whole face as he turned to go into the house, and made him look handsome. Although he was not a very well-educated young man, and although when he talked he did not always use the best of English, still the slow, even tone in which he spoke his words and the rare smile with which they were often accompanied, took the sharp edge from what would otherwise have grated on the refined ear, and made one feel that here was true heart culture at least, if there was not overmuch education.

It was pleasant, too, to see the tenderness with which he approached the bed of his young invalid brother, after he had removed the great straw hat which covered his well-shaped head, and stood some minutes at the kitchen sink, making a half-way toilet before the cracked looking-glass.

"Harley, I've some good news for you," he said. "Lois is coming home to-night on the evening express, and her father says he's sure she'll run right over here the first thing. Maybe she'll come in the morning."

The joy of the young invalid was quite apparent. He had very few pleasures in his monotonous life. Ever since the scarlet fever had attacked him, several years ago, his had been but a weary, painful existence.

He was not much more than thirteen years old, but his life of pain had made him old in many ways beyond his years, while the constant necessary reliance upon others had kept him quite a child too. He had the same dark, handsome eyes as his brother, but his face, though a trifle thin and pinched with the pain he had suffered, was beautiful as any girl's.

"Oh, Frank, I'm so glad!" he exclaimed, catching his brother's hand and squeezing it. "Now she'll have more stories to tell, and maybe some new plans for me. I'm so tired of all the old ones, and besides I've outgrown them. Three months is a long time when one has to spend it on the bed, you know, and can use the nights to live in as well as the days— that is, most of them"—and he smiled a sorry little smile.

"On the evening express did you say she was coming?" he asked again suddenly as if a new idea had struck him. "Then why couldn't you carry me into the other room for just a little while and let me watch it go by? It would be such fun to see it and then to think that there was someone I knew in the lighted-up cars. I've watched it before, you know, but I didn't ever have any one in them to feel that way about. Why, it would be 'most as good as going in a train again myself, as I did when I was such a little fellow before I was hurt, with father. I can remember real well about how the cars looked, and if I could see the express go by to-night and could think she was in it, maybe I could imagine myself in those cars whirling along beside her, coming home from the city like any boy. Say, Franklin, you will, won't you? It won't hurt me to be moved to-night, a bit, for I've had a real good day," he finished triumphantly, and then looked up to his brother's face with such pleading in his eyes as could not be resisted, albeit the brother's were so full of tears that he was forced to turn his head the other way for a moment.

"If mother says so, Harley," he managed to get out, and then strode from the room to find the mother and choke down his rising feelings.

Harley had his wish, although the troubled mother doubted the wisdom of it when she saw the fever into which her boy worked himself before the train did finally rush by. And then it was such a passing pleasure, with all his imaginings of himself on board. A few sparks, a few shrieks, a roar, a rush, a bright, quick glancing of lighted windows with dim figures in them, and then all was over, and Harley could scarcely get to sleep, so excited was he.

He was awake very early the next morning. He knew the colors of the sunrise well, and could tell you all about them, for he had watched them many times from his window,

after long nights of weary hours, which it had
seemed to him would never end. He watched
the pink bars of the sky slowly turn to gold,
and then melt away into a glory that burst over
the world and filled everything, even his room,
and brightened his pale face for a little. Then
the world waked and went to work and things
began. Harley might hope for Lois to come
soon, for had she not been his friend for so
long, and did she not love him dearly? She
surely would come over directly after breakfast. And Lois did not disappoint him. She
came while it was still early, with a great spray
of chestnut burs in her hand, that the frost had
opened and robbed of their nuts just to show
the world what a pretty velvet lining was
inside.

Lois had not exactly a beautiful face when
you considered it carefully; her skin was pink,
and her eyes blue, with yellow lashes, and her
hands just the least mite freckled, like her
father's, but the eyes were bright and sweet,
and the lashes had somehow caught and tan-
gled a sunbeam into them, and the hands were
quick and graceful, nevertheless; besides Lois
had hair—wonderful hair! It began by being
red like her father's, but the glory of the
sunlight was in it to mellow it, and the soft

brown richness of her mother's had toned it down, until the red only shone through in little glints, and made it the most beautiful halo of soft, rippling light about her head; so that when you considered her hair, Lois was lovely. Harley thought her very beautiful, and I am not sure but his brother Franklin held the same opinion.

"And now, Lois," said Harley, when the greetings were over, and they had settled down to an old-time talk, "begin! What will you tell me first? Let me see. Begin with the nicest thing first. What was the nicest thing you saw in all the time you were gone?"

Lois raised her eyes a little above their level, and put on her thoughtful expression. Harley liked to see her so, and feasted his eyes upon her as she studied the ceiling, thinking how good it was to have her back with him again.

But Lois's eyes were beginning to brighten and a smile crept over her face which Harley knew was the harbinger of some good thought or story.

"I think the convention was the best of all," she said, bringing her eyes back to his face, full of pleasant memories for him to read.

"Convention! What convention?" asked Harley almost impatiently, "and how could a convention be the pleasantest thing in a visit to a big town?"

"But it was," said Lois emphatically, "the very best thing of all. I think if I had to choose between the whole of the rest of my visit and those three days of convention I wouldn't have stopped a minute to think, I would have chosen the convention—at least, that's the way I'd do, now I've been to it."

Harley looked puzzled. He could not understand why a convention should be particularly interesting to a girl, but he had unlimited faith in Lois and her taste.

"Was it politics, or a firemen's convention? And did they—why, I suppose they had a great many parades, didn't they? Was that why it was so nice?" he asked, trying to understand.

"Oh, no, indeed!" said Lois, laughing. "It wasn't politics nor firemen nor Farmers' Alliance nor any of those things. It's a long story, and I'll have to begin at the beginning. It was the State convention of the Y.P.S.C.E. Do you know what those letters mean?" and she stopped to watch the color deepen in Harley's cheek and his eyes shine as he tried to guess what the mystic letters could mean, but after he had made several unsuccessful attempts she went on.

"It means Young People's Society of Christian Endeavor," she said, naming each word on a finger of her hand, and nodding triumphantly as she finished. "Do you know about it?"

"No," said Harley. "It sounds stupid. I can't see how you could like it so much," and there was almost a quiver of disappointment about his mouth.

But Lois hastened to take up her story and make its scenes live again before the eager eyes of her small listener.

2

"IT'S a very big society," she began; "there's one all over everywhere pretty near. They even have one in Japan, they say. It's a society of the young folks all working for Christ. That's what Endeavor means, you see. It's a long story, so if you don't understand all I say you better ask questions, for I may leave out some. All the young folks get together first and say, 'We'll have a society,' and then they take the pledge and the constitution and"—

"What's the pledge and constitution?" interrupted Harley.

"I don't know much about the constitution," said Lois. "I guess it's just their laws; but the pledge I've learned by heart:

"'Trusting in the Lord Jesus Christ for strength, I promise Him that I will strive to do whatever He would like to have me do; that I will pray to Him and read the Bible every day, and that, just so far as I know how, throughout my whole life, I will endeavor to lead a Christian life.'

"That's the first half. I didn't learn the rest. It's about being at all the meetings and helping them along, and always going to the consecration meeting once a month, unless you have an excuse you can give to God. I didn't think it was worth while to learn that part, because we haven't any society here and I don't suppose we ever shall have. They don't take to such things in this town, but I thought the first half of that pledge anybody could take and be a society by one's self, so I have written it down and signed my name to it, and I'm trying to be a Young People's Society of Christian Endeavor all by myself. Well, about once in so often—once a year, I guess it is—they have a convention. There's a great big one of all the societies in the country, in some big city—that's what they call the 'National'—but this wasn't one of those. This was a State convention. That means just the societies in that State, you know. Mrs. Brant said she invited me to come to town early in the season so that I could be there to the convention, because she thought I would enjoy it; and I did, ever so much. Well, the first meeting was in the evening, and they began to come—the delegates—along in the afternoon, from the trains that came in from all directions. Maybe you'd see a young man with a satchel, and then three girls, and then two or three youngish boys, and you'd run to the window and say, 'There come some delegates! I wonder if they're the ones that'll come here to our house!' You see Mrs. Brant kept three of them, two young men, and a girl that roomed with me, and I got pretty well acquainted with her and she told me all about their society at home and"—

"But what's a delegate?" interrupted Harley again.

"Oh! they're the folks each society sends to represent them. The whole society couldn't come, of course, because it would cost too much and they couldn't all be entertained, and then some of them would have to stay at home any way, I suppose; so each society sends two or three of its members, and they call them delegates. Some of the delegates were very nice. They all wore badges just like the Grand Army men when they go to a big meeting, only these had Y.P.S.C.E. on them in big letters and the name of the town they came from, and some of them had a motto. It was ever so nice to study their badges and say to them, 'You live in Newtown, don't you? Why, I have a cousin there. Did you ever see her?' I heard from two people I used to know, that way. It was real exciting that first night before I got used to it. Mrs. Brant had raised biscuits and doughnuts and thin slices of ham and some of her nicest preserves for supper, and there was the best table-cloth and the biggest napkins, and the whole house looked so 'receptiony.' The three delegates looked as if they enjoyed it, too, when they came downstairs with their hair all combed, and their eyes shining as if they'd just got to the front hall of Heaven and expected to be shown a good way inside before the next three days were over. We had to hurry through supper, for the first bell began to ring early, and it kind of made us all uneasy to get there and begin, we'd heard so much about it and talked it over so long. I'd meant to take real solid enjoyment eating one of those doughnuts, for Mrs. Brant does make such lovely ones, but I was so in a hurry to get to meeting that I actually didn't finish mine.

"The first thing that night was a sermon, and it was a grand one. I do wish we could have such preaching here in Parkerstown. It just made me feel as if I wasn't any kind of a Christian, though I have been a member of the church for four years. Why, all those young folks are doing so much and living so differently from what I am, that I felt all sort of left out. I haven't remembered much of the sermon itself—not the words—but that's the way it made me feel, and I never shall get away from the feeling that came that night that I mustn't waste any more time living the way I'd been doing.

"When we got home, after we'd had a talk awhile in the parlor with the delegates, and they'd gone to bed, we got breakfast as near ready as we could the night before, so we could go to the meeting at six o'clock in the morning. When I heard about that meeting I thought it was a dreadfully silly idea to begin so early, and I made up my mind that whatever else I went to, I wouldn't go to that meeting. I thought I'd have enough without it, but Mrs. Brant said she wanted me to go; that they said it was one of the best meetings of the whole thing, and I felt a little curious about it after the delegates began to talk so much of it, and so we decided to go, and slip out ahead to have breakfast all ready for them when they came back. And we did. You ask about parades. They weren't exactly any parades, only when church was out they looked a little that way, everybody with badges, you know, but before those morning meetings there was just a procession of folks going. It was interesting to see them. I stood in the door and watched while the last bell was ringing, and the people came hurrying from all directions. There was a family opposite that Mrs. Brant says never go to church, and it was very funny to see them come to the door, and the man poked his head out of the upper window to see if there was a fire or anything that people were all out so early and the bells were ringing. They found out after a few hours, though, that the bell would keep on ringing all day.

"It was the most beautiful meeting that I had ever been to, then. The leader read the twenty-third psalm, about 'The Lord is my shepherd,' you know, and then we sang, 'I was a wandering sheep,' and the leader asked them all to pray, and they did, ever so many of them. I think there were twenty or thirty prayers right in a minute or two, and they didn't try to pray long and ask for everything in the world at once, but each one had some little thing he wanted for himself, or for them all, that he asked for. Then they sang, 'There were ninety and nine,' and the leader told them that as there was but half an hour for the meeting any way, that they must all be quick and short, or everybody wouldn't have a chance, and they all were.

"A girl spoke up just as soon as they got through, and said she had been thinking while he read the verses, how she had heard that it was the lambs that kept close to the shepherd that he cared for most tenderly. He found nice things for them to eat, and he took them up and carried them when they were worn out, and when there was danger they always felt safe, and she thought it was a good deal so with following Jesus: the ones that kept close to Him had an easier time and loved Him better than those that only followed far away. Then one of our young men delegates recited a beautiful poem, and it was so pretty I asked him to write it out for me. I can only remember a few lines of it, but you shall have it all to read when I unpack my trunk. It began like this:

> "I was wandering and weary
> When my Saviour came unto me;
> For the ways of sin grew dreary,

And the world had ceased to woo me:
And I thought I heard Him say,
As He came along His way,
'O silly souls! come near Me;
My sheep should never fear Me;
I am the Shepherd true.'

"*He took me on His shoulder,*
and tenderly He kissed me;
He bade my love be bolder,
And said how He had missed me;
And I'm sure I heard Him say,
As He came along His way,
'O silly souls! come near Me;
My sheep should never fear Me;
I am the Shepherd true.'

"There was an old man sitting way back, and he said, right after that, that he didn't want to take up the time of the young folks as he knew he was an old man, but he had been a shepherd himself once, and he knew all about sheep. He said they wouldn't ever lie down until they had had enough to eat and were quite comfortable, and that he had been thinking that when Jesus Christ made people 'to lie down in pleasant pastures,' that it meant that he always fed them and made them com-

fortable and happy first. There were ever so
many other pretty little things said about
sheep and lambs, and some Bible verses and
bits of poetry recited, and some more prayers
and singing, and I really didn't think we had
been in the church ten minutes, when the
leader said the time had come to close.

"We all got back to the church again as soon
after breakfast as we could to the business
meeting. I had made up my mind by that time
that those young folks could make even business interesting, if they could do so much with
a half-hour prayer meeting. Besides, I intended
to find out all I could about this queer society.
The business was just as interesting as could be.
They had a bright, quick man for president,
and he made things spin; and they settled ever
so many questions, and made a dozen committees to attend to things in less than no time,
and then he called for the reports from societies. It was just the most amazing thing I ever
did, to sit there and hear all those young boys
and girls and men and women get up, one after
another, and tell of what their society was
doing, how many members it had, when it was
formed, how it had grown, and all sorts of
things about it. They kept calling for new
places all the time, and I just expected they

would call for Parkerstown next, and I would have to get up and say we hadn't any society here, and never had even heard of it. I was so ashamed of Parkerstown that I didn't know what to do. But they didn't call for it. That afternoon there were two speeches about doing work for Christ, and there were papers five minutes long from different people, telling the best ways of working on the different committees they have in the society, Lookout and Social and Prayer meeting and all those things. I can't remember the rest of them, but I have a constitution at home in my trunk, and that will tell you what they all mean if you want to see it. They gave some nice ideas that made me wish we had a society here, so we could do some of the things they told about.

"It was great fun in the evening when the secretary came. He is the great secretary, you know, of the 'National,' and they felt very proud to think he had promised to come to their convention, because he is so busy that he can't always go to all the conventions. He came in on the evening train, and came right down to the church without even a chance to wash his hands. We were singing when he came in, because we had been kind of waiting along for the train to come, and at the end of the verses we all waved our handkerchiefs at him as he came up to the platform. He was a splendid-looking young man, real young; you would hardly have thought him more than a boy at first, though when you looked at him closer you saw that he was a good deal older, and he didn't talk like any boy, I can tell you. He just stood up there and made everybody love him at first. He told us how glad he was to see us, and how he had come a long journey just to be with us. Then we were all so glad he had come, and began to wonder how we had gotten along with our convention so far without him and called it a good time; and we felt right away how sorry we should be when the next day was over and we should have to say good-by to him. He talked beautifully. I wish I could tell you all the stories he told us, and what wonderful things he said we could do if each one did his part. I have some of the things down in my little blank book, and when I come over next time I'll bring it, and then I can tell you more of his talk. He didn't talk very long, and then we all went home and went to sleep.

"The next morning's prayer meeting was just as good as the first one, and a little better because the secretary was there, and somehow he made us feel as if Jesus Christ were a good deal nearer to us since he came, because he seemed to love Him so very much. The next day there were reports and business and talks and a question-drawer where everybody asked questions on paper and the secretary answered them, and there was a story read, a beautiful story. I'll tell you that, all by itself, another time. It's too long for now. It was a Christian Endeavor story, too; everything was Christian Endeavor. Early in the evening there was a big reception in the town hall. Everybody went and shook hands with the secretary. I was introduced to him too, and he smiled just as cordially at me as he did to the people he stayed with and must have known a great deal better. Then about nine o'clock we all went in a procession to the church for the closing consecration meeting.

"Why, Harley, I never went to anything like that meeting! I can't begin to tell you anything about it. There were almost a hundred prayers in just about ten minutes. The singing was so sweet; everybody was so much in earnest; and it seemed as if Jesus was right there in the room waiting to give a blessing to everyone, to me just as much as any one else. Every body talked too, and told what the convention had done for them, and how it had helped them. I had to tell too, just a little word. I felt as if it would be ungrateful to go away from that meeting without saying how happy I felt for having been allowed to be there, and how I wanted so much to belong to that society, only we hadn't any to belong to, but I thought I would try by myself; and then some one came to me afterwards and told me he hoped I would begin a society, that I would likely find some one else to help, and that we would have a Christian Endeavor in our town before the next year's convention. Of course I didn't tell them what a hard place Parkerstown is, but I did wish with all my heart I had a society to come home to and join. I've been going to the one in Lewiston all the time I've been there, and they made me join; so I'm really a member after all.

"Well, the delegates mostly left by the midnight train, and we all went down to the station and had another reception and sort of praise-meeting there. The strangers seemed a little astonished at the queer set of young people who were singing and talking about religion. I heard one man say he never came across any like them before, but I guess it didn't do him any harm, for he threw away his cigar and went and had a long talk with the secretary. Aren't you tired now, Harley, and don't you want me to stop?"

No, Harley was not tired one bit, and he had a great many questions to ask. They were answered patiently and carefully by one who had such an intense interest in the subject that it was a pleasure to her to explain even the driest detail.

3

"IF you can be a society all by yourself why couldn't I join?" asked Harley at last. "I should like to be a society. I couldn't do anything of course, but it would be nice to say I belonged to something like other boys. You said there were two kinds of members, didn't you? What are they? Tell me again. Why couldn't I be one of that other kind?"

"Yes; we have two kinds of members," answered Lois, unconsciously using the pronoun "we" in that connection for the first time, "active and associate, but the associate members are not much. They can't even vote. It is just to get hold of people and make them feel that they belong, you know. A real member ought to be an active member, I should think. You see the associate members are not Christians. An associate member is a kind of a 'half-way' thing, any way. Why couldn't you be an active one?"

"Why, what would I have to do? I don't 'act' any. I just have to lie here and 'be,'" said the boy, with a quiver about his mouth.

"Oh, don't, Harley dear!" cried Lois, with tears in her eyes. "Yes, you could be an active member. You could give yourself to Jesus and sign the active membership pledge and keep it just as well as I can, and you would find lots of little bits of work to do for Christ right here in your own room."

Harley looked thoughtful and shook his head.

"I'm afraid I couldn't be much of a Christian," he said, "for you see, sometimes when my head aches so bad I'm cross. I have to be, and then it kind of gets the hurt out a little if I talk scolding to them, and make them give me my own way. But maybe I might. What did you say was the pledge again? I'd like to have it to think about a while. It would be nice to be a member of something. If I was 'active' we could have business meetings and I could vote, couldn't I? That would be lots of fun. But it wouldn't be right to think about that part of it unless I was really willing to sign my pledge and keep it, would it?"

"No;" Lois admitted that she did not think it would. "I'll tell you what we can do, Harley," she said, "I can't remember the whole pledge, but I'll write out the part that I said off to you and you can think that over, and when I go home I will write to the place in Boston where they keep pledge-cards, and we'll each have a pledge-card to keep. It will be nice, I think, if we are going to be a society. You will like that, won't you?"

Harley showed his appreciation of it by the brightness of his eyes.

So the first half of the pledge was written out and placed under Harley's pillow for further consideration. Lois said she must go home, and Harley followed her with wistful looks, then closed his eyes to think of all she had told him, and to sleep a little while with pleasant dreams of it.

It was three or four days before Lois found time to run up to see her little friend again. He had awaited her coming with great impatience, and now he drew the rumpled slip of paper from under his cushion and said as she entered the room:

"I think I can sign it, Lois. I've thought it all over and I'll try to keep it. You see, that first sentence helped me a good deal. It says, 'Trusting in the Lord Jesus Christ for strength.' I thought I couldn't be good all the time, but if I trust in Him to help me when I can't, why then I've nothing else to do but be as good as I can and then He'll do the rest. It isn't like promising some one else, either, that wouldn't understand when I was doing my best, and when the pain was so hard that I had to cry just a little. He'll always know when I'm doing my best, and it's Him I'll have to promise and not any one else. It doesn't seem hard to do what He wants me to do, for that isn't much now, but to lie still and be patient, and be willing to give up when I can't have what I want. I think I can promise that. And then of course I can read the Bible a little while, and pray. I haven't always done it. Sometimes I would think it wasn't any use, and sometimes there was something I would want to do instead, like hearing a story or thinking about some plan I had made to amuse myself, and so I would forget to pray, but I guess I will join, Lois, if there isn't anything else in the pledge to promise."

Lois bent down and kissed the pure, white forehead and, looking into the eager earnest eyes, felt that she would have a true little Christian for her co-laborer in the Christian Endeavor Society.

"The pledge-cards have come, Harley," she said, as she took her seat by his bed. "Didn't they come quickly? I ran right over with them because I thought you'd be in a hurry to see them. They came on the noon mail."

Harley reached an eager hand for the card and read it slowly, his face growing sober as he read.

"What kind of meetings does it mean I must be 'present at'?" he asked, "and what is a 'consecration' meeting?"

Lois explained carefully about the prayer meetings and the monthly consecration meeting at which the roll was called, and each member responded to his name by telling of his progress during the past month, or by repeating a verse from the Bible.

"Could you and I have prayer meetings here in my room, do you mean, Lois? And, Lois, who would pray?"

Lois had thought of these questions a little and had made up her mind to do her duty and try to begin a Christian Endeavor Society right here, but it was nevertheless with beating heart that she answered:

"Yes, I think we might, Harley, and I suppose if there was no one else here, you and I would have to pray."

Harley considered this a moment, "Of course," said he, "you could pray. Maybe I'd get so I could too, a little, but I don't know how very well. Anyhow, I'd try if God wants me to do that."

"Then we'll be a society. Here's a constitution, and I've subscribed for the Golden Rule. That's the paper that's all about Christian Endeavor Societies, and you shall have it to read every week. I had it sent to you so you would get it as soon as it came. I thought it would interest you."

"Oh, thank you, Lois dear! How good you are to me! I shall not have any more stupid days now you've come home. The summer was so very long without you! How nice it will be to have a paper to read myself and all about our society!"

"And now when shall we have our first meeting?" asked Lois.

After much discussion it was decided to hold the meetings on Sunday afternoons at three o'clock.

"Because," said Harley, "this would be something like going to church, and I have wanted to go to church for so long. Besides, I have great trouble with Sundays. They are quite long and there hasn't been much I could do with them. Franklin reads to me a good deal, but he always takes a walk in the woods on Sundays, and I don't think he quite enjoys reading the things that mother thinks fit Sunday best; so, if you please, I'd like it on Sunday afternoon."

The paper arrived before the first Sunday meeting, and was eagerly devoured by its owner. He read to himself as long as they would allow him, and then every member of the family was pressed into service until he knew the matter of that week's issue pretty thoroughly. He had a very clear idea of what a Christian Endeavor prayer meeting should be, and he had gained much information about the various committees and their workings.

"We can't be, just us two, Lois," he announced when she came in Sunday afternoon. "I've been reading about it, and if we are a society at all, we'll have to go to work and get in some more. Besides, we need a president and secretary and ever so many committees. There's the prayer meeting committee and the lookout. I guess we don't need a social one yet, for we'll be social enough, just us two. But the lookout committee seems to be the beginning of every thing. We'll have to have a business meeting. We don't want to have that on Sunday, and we'd better have one right off Monday, and fix these things. Now begin. You'll have to lead the meeting to-day because you know how, and you must tell me what to do all along. I've been reading up about these things. Did you know there is a subject already picked out for every week? I think we'd better take that, don't you? It will be nice to think we are having the same kind of a meeting they are having everywhere else, and we can pretend there are more folks here, and pick out things for them to say and read."

Lois began her first meeting with a trembling heart. It was hard for her to do such a thing even before this little boy. But she read a few verses and then knelt down by Harley's bed and prayed: "Dear Jesus, wilt Thou bless this little society of two, and help us to know how to work for Thee as the other larger societies are doing? For Jesus' sake. Amen." And Harley followed without being asked, with:

"Dear Jesus, I thank Thee for sending me word about this society. Please help me to be a good member and keep my pledge, and show me how I can work. Amen."

It was not a very long meeting, but it was a good one. The great army of Christian Endeavors over the land, if they had been permitted to look in upon the two with the open Bible between them, might perhaps not have felt much inspiration from the sight; but there nevertheless was, in that small meeting, the true Christian Endeavor spirit. They had claimed the promise that "where two or three of you shall gather in my name, I will be with them," and God's Spirit was indeed there.

"I have thought of Sallie Elder," said Harley, when the solemn Christian Endeavor parting words, "The Lord watch between me and thee when we are absent one from another" had been repeated, and they had pronounced their first prayer meeting concluded. "Sallie Elder doesn't know what to do with Sunday. She told me so the other day when she was over here. I guess we could get her in. I could send a note to her all about it. I should like to write it, and Pepper could take it to her. Do you think, Lois, that it would be wicked to put Pepper on the lookout committee? If he does part of the work he ought to belong, oughtn't he? It wouldn't be wrong, would it, Lois?"

Now Pepper was a very homely little dog, who lay curled in a heap at Harley's feet during the meeting, fast asleep, and at the mention of his name he pricked up his ears, opened his bright little wistful eyes up at the two, and thumped his tail pleadingly as much as to say, "Do take me in; I'll be a very good dog."

It was finally decided that Pepper should be a sort of *ex-officio* member of the committee, and should be sent after Sallie Elder before the next prayer meeting.

Sallie accepted the invitation with delight and became an associate member immediately. Lois was glad at this addition; but when, next Sunday, Harley announced that his brother Franklin had asked for admittance to the society, or at least to the meetings, her heart beat fast, and there was consternation in her face. Admit Franklin Winters to their meetings! How could they! He was not a Christian. Indeed, he was known to have said many things which led one to think he did not much believe in the Bible. Lois had always liked him very much, but she was afraid of him. He might make fun of their meetings. But even as she thought that, her heart told her he would not do such a thing as that. Perhaps he only wished to come there to please his little brother. But who would pray if Franklin came? Surely she could not.

She had never prayed aloud before in her life until she went to Lewiston, and there only once or twice. It had been a little trial to think of having Sallie added to their number, but she had decided to bear that for the sake of the good they might be able to do, but now to have this young man come—oh! it would be dreadful. It would be an impossibility to pray, and yet what could she say to Harley? Moreover, it appeared that Franklin was waiting in the other room for admittance. Lois must answer quickly.

"Why, Harley," she said, and her voice trembled as she looked down and fumbled with some papers between the leaves of her Bible, "I am afraid your brother wouldn't enjoy it. It's just us, you know, and"—

"Oh, yes, he would!" broke in Harley. "I told him all about it, and he said, all of his own accord, that he wished we would let him come, and his eyes looked real 'want to' when he said it, and he asked ever so many questions about it; so he knows just what it is. He said he thought if Sallie came that he might, and that he'd like to ever so much."

Before Lois had time to reply Franklin himself appeared at the door with Sallie, and his pleasant eyes were upon Lois's face while he asked:

"You are going to let me come, too, aren't you? Harley said he thought you would be glad to have an addition. I can't do much, to be sure, but I think I might manage to conduct myself as honorably as Pepper here," and he gave the dog a pat on the head, which was highly appreciated.

4

FRANKLIN sat down then, and there was
nothing for Lois to do but submit, although
she would gladly have fled the house and her
newly fledged Christian Endeavor Society and
never come back any more. Harley was to lead
the meeting, so she had nothing to do but
await developments, but she sat with her eyes
down and her whole body in a quiver. Harley
asked her almost immediately to pray for the
opening of the meeting. She knelt down with
not a thought in her mind and scarcely a desire
in her heart, except that she might be helped
to get out of this trying situation, and the help
came. "Thine ears shall hear a word behind
thee, saying, 'This is the way, walk ye in it, . . .
Now therefore go, and I will be with thy
mouth, and teach thee what thou shalt say.'"

Surely those promises were fulfilled for her that day. She had not known what to say nor how to say anything indeed, but the young man who knelt across the room listening was amazed, and found himself wondering if it was really Lois Peters who was talking in that sweet voice, apparently to some One who stood close beside her, and in whom she seemed to have the utmost confidence. He seemed to feel that he was being prayed about too, although his name was not uttered, and for the first time in his life he believed that there was something in religion which he did not understand, a power that reached into the heart-life as nothing else could do. Harley felt the influence of that prayer too, as he took up the petition where Lois left off:

"Please, dear God, we thank Thee that we have some new members to our society. Help them to get to be active members pretty soon. Let Pepper be a good member, if he is only a dog. He can run around and do the errands I could do if I were like other boys. Amen."

The little dog curled up on the bed beside his young master, opened his eyes and raised his head inquiringly at the mention of his name, but seeing Harley's eyes closed, he rested his cold nose confidingly against Harley's clasped hands and closed his own eyes until the Amen, when he gave a soft whine of satisfaction and settled down among the pillows again. Franklin's eyes were wet with tears when he raised his face from his hands, and Lois's face was grave, but little Sallie Elder sat immovable on the edge of her chair, with wide-open eyes, throughout the entire service, uncertain just what to call this strange performance to which she had been invited. It was not until Harley read slowly and carefully a story from the Bible that she began to be interested, and by and by when the reading was over and the meeting thrown open for remarks, she was persuaded into repeating her one Bible verse: "Suffer little children to come unto me."

Franklin, too, had consented to read a verse if he were allowed to come, and not being very familiar with the Bible himself, Harley had selected it for him.

That was the beginning of the Parkerstown Christian Endeavor Society. It is not needful that you should know what was read or said at that meeting. There was nothing original or remarkable in it. You might think it very commonplace, but to those who were gathered there it seemed not so. They had caught the spirit of Christian Endeavor, and even Franklin felt that there was a power there, greater than any other which he knew. He promised to come again if they would let him, and even volunteered to become a temporary member of the lookout committee until some more worthy members should come in. He would that week agree to bring in at least two to the next meeting. Lois's heart began to swell with the thought of a real society right there in Parkerstown, albeit she had scarcely gotten over her panic at the rapid development of her small scheme. It was something to be thought about and prayed over, this, actually planning to speak and pray before people like Franklin Winters, every week. She was not sure she would be able to do it, though she recognized that a power higher than her own had helped her that afternoon; but would He always help? Surely He had promised, but—she must get away by herself and think it over. Happy for Lois that she had learned lately to think such things over upon her knees. The Lord presides over decisions made there, and so it was with a less fearful heart that she came to the next meeting, having herself prevailed upon three young girls to come with her.

Harley had been made president. First, because they thought it would please him, but he proved such a good president, with so many wise and original little plans for the growth of the society, that they came to feel after all that they could not have chosen more wisely. For Harley read all he could get hold of, and he knew all about the great Christian Endeavor Society; he knew all its principles and the wisest ways of working; he knew more about it than all the rest of Parkerstown put together. Moreover, he had time to think and plan and, best of all, to pray, and to grow, in this thinking and planning and praying, daily like Jesus Christ. They all saw the change in his life, even patient as it had been heretofore. There was a wondrous beauty growing in that face that spoke of an inward peace, and a sweet wisdom that had touched the child-heart and caused it to open like a flower.

It came about very gradually, the addition to the society. First, Franklin brought two boys, farm hands from a neighbor's house, and then little Sallie coaxed her older sister, and then all grew interested and the meetings became larger until it was hard to find chairs enough in the square white house by the roadside, and until Harley's little bedroom off the sitting-room became too small to contain all the members.

"Father," said Harley one evening, when he had been lying quite still for a long time with his eyes closed, so that they all began to step softly and talk in low tones, thinking him asleep, "I wish you would take me into the big south room to-morrow. I haven't been in there in two years, I guess, and I want to see it. I have a plan. Perhaps you won't like it, and if you don't I will not coax; but, father, I should like to go in there and see it."

"You shall go, my son," said the father, who could not deny Harley anything in these days. "What is your plan, my boy?"

"Well, father, if you and mother don't like it, I won't make any fuss, but it's something I think would be very nice. Do you think mother cares very much about that south room? I know it's the parlor, and there's all the best things in there, but she doesn't use it much only on Christmas days, and not much then nowadays. It seems too bad to have it using itself up in the dark when it would be so nice for our society. I shouldn't think it would hurt things very much—just once a week—would it? Or couldn't I have it for my bedroom and you move the things in here and have this for the parlor? Do you think it is a very ridiculous plan, father? Because if you do, you and mother, why, I said I wouldn't coax, but I'd like to have you think it over very hard before you say," he said pleadingly.

And so, after much calculation and some changing of household plans, with a few tears mingled by father and mother, it is true—tears of love for their afflicted little boy—the plan was carried out, and the front parlor of the Winters' household became the headquarters of the Parkerstown Christian Endeavor Society. It is true that the room had not been much used as a parlor, and that it afforded ample accommodation for the meetings of the society.

"In fact," said father Winters, "we don't need it and they do, and what Harley wants will please us better than anything else, any way."

There was much bustle of preparation after the decision was made. Franklin agreed to give as his part enough cane-seat chairs to accommodate the members. Some one sent a fine engraving of Father Endeavor Clark, Lois brought over a large copy of the United Society Pledge, neatly framed, to hang over Harley's couch, and together she and Harley planned little decorations to make the room look home-like and yet "churchified," as Harley said. A great monogram C. E., was made from evergreen and hung in the center of one wall, surrounded by the motto, "For Christ and the Church." Another wall contained the motto, "One is your Master, even Christ; and all ye are brethren." Harley made Lois describe the mottoes she had seen at the convention in Lewiston, and they made theirs as much like them as possible. When the motto, "For Christ and the Church," was put up, Harley lay thinking long about it. He didn't see how he could be working for the Church at all. But the end of his thoughts was that he wanted the new minister asked to attend the meetings. The minister was invited, and came with a glad heart. He had heard of this society with thankfulness, but had not thought it best to come until invited. Now he became one with the young people, and helped them along more than they knew. He grew to love the little president much as did every one else, and came frequently to see him, finding that in this young disciple there was much of the spirit of Jesus, and that he might sit at his feet and gather inspiration and new love and faith from conversation with this sweet, trusting child.

The work of this society was carried on according to the most approved methods. No suggestion passed by unheeded. Everything, too, was talked over carefully with the minister, to see whether in their particular society such and such measures were expedient. Every member had a pledge-card. There were cards from the National Headquarters for the different committees to use in their work, and topic cards and everything else that could be thought of; for when Harley expressed a wish for a simple little thing like that to work with, there were plenty to see that it was granted; and so it came about that there was not in all the State, a society better fitted out for work in all departments, than the one at Parkerstown.

Harley had one thing of which he was very proud. The minister brought it to him one day when he came to see him. It was a Christian Endeavor scarf-pin of solid gold; and how Harley loved that pin! He looked at it for hours at a time thinking what it meant; he held it in the rays of sunlight that lay across his bed; he wore it pinned on the breast of his dressing-gown with pleasure, and showed it to every one that came to see him.

"It seems to shine brighter than any other gold thing," he said one day. "I wonder what makes it. Is it because it is for Christ?"

The meetings were large in these days, and very solemn ones. A good many of the Parkerstown young people were beginning to find out what it is to belong to Jesus Christ, and many others were seeking Him. Even the new big room was full every Sunday afternoon, and the songs that filled the air and floated out to the street often drew in outsiders who were taking a little walk or who had nothing else to do. Lois had sacrificed her organ to the cause, though it was not a sacrifice, but given gladly, and Franklin had brought it over himself, so they had good rousing singing and plenty of it, and Harley would lie on his little couch by the desk and look at the organ with admiring eyes, feeling that it lent a dignity of the church to the modest room.

But there were days, and growing more frequent now, when the little couch by the light desk was empty, and the young president of this society was unable to be moved in to the meeting, but must lie in the darkened bedroom beyond, with the door closed, and suffer. At first they thought the meetings must be adjourned when Harley was not able to be there, because the noise would trouble him, and because they felt they could not do without him, until he begged so hard that all should go on as usual that it was tried as an experiment, in hushed voices, and without music. But Harley missed that at once and sent word for them to sing:

> *At the cross, at the cross, where I first saw the*
> *   light,*
> *And the burden of my heart rolled away,*
> *It was there by faith I received my sight,*
> *And now I am happy all the day.*

He said the singing rested him. So, after that they went on as usual, only when the president was not there, there was a more earnest feeling manifest in all the members, and much praying done that the dear boy might be relieved from his sufferings. Some who had not cared much about the meetings heretofore seemed strangely touched by the thought that the little, patient sufferer was lying there thinking of them and praying for them.

5

IT was the evening of the day after one of these sad, painful Sabbaths. Lois and his brother Franklin were sitting by Harley's bed. They had been telling him about the meeting as he had asked them. Franklin let Lois do much of the talking, he only helping her out here and there when she forgot what came next, or called upon him to know who was present. He was not yet an active member, and apparently no nearer being a Christian than when the society was first organized. He came in regularly to the meetings and did whatever he was asked to do, even to reading a verse of Harley's selection, but he never selected one himself, and always kept in the background as much as possible. People said he was doing it all for his little brother's sake, and no one dared approach him upon the subject or even urge him to do more. Very few remembered to pray for him I think, there were so many others worse than he, they thought. But Lois was praying, and so was his brother. Many a night when he could not sleep he lay and talked with God and asked Him to make Franklin love Him.

"I want to tell you something," said Harley suddenly rousing from deep silence into which they had fallen. "I have seen something, and I think you would like to know about it. I should like it if you should see such a thing to have you tell me about it. It was last Sunday when you were at meeting. The pain in my eyes was so bad that I had to close them and my head ached very badly, so that I couldn't even have the bedroom door open to hear your voices in the room, but had to close my ears, too, to bear the pain. I could just hear the sound of the song you were singing. I do not remember what it was, but it was very sweet, though it seemed far away, and it grew further away, and further, until it suddenly seemed to turn and come back again and burst into the sweetest, clearest music you ever heard. It was like, and yet it was not like, the music in our meetings. It was such as that would be if every voice was perfect, perhaps the sort of singing they have in Heaven, though I never knew before that any singing could be sweeter than we have in our meetings; but of course Heaven has everything better.

"Well, this singing, although it was very near and loud, didn't make my head ache a bit harder, and even seemed to rest my back; at least I forgot it was aching. There was a light all around, too, and I could look up without its hurting my eyes. I didn't think how strange that was then, but just listened to the music and looked at the light. It took a shape in some clouds that were far off and yet all around—you see you were not there and so I can't quite explain it all, because there wasn't time for me to understand everything about it, and there was so much else to see. The light grew brighter and brighter and broadened out at the top as though a hundred suns were shining through one spot, and there was a long, sharp, golden crack in the clouds below, and the light changed and broadened and shaped and brightened in such a strange way until suddenly I thought of the shape of my Christian Endeavor pin, and then all at once I saw the letters at the top C. E., and the long sharp ray of light was the pin, and there it was in the clouds all gold, and growing 'golder' every minute, until I thought I couldn't look any longer; but I had to, because it was so beautiful. And then I saw that the line that made the pin was only a break in the clouds, where the light from Heaven—it must have been Heaven— shone through. Above, in the large, bright letters was a real opening into such light as you never saw before, not even when the sun sets; and then there came angels, hurrying out of the letters and down through the narrow opening and everywhere towards me, and more were beyond up there in the brightness. I watched them come out through the opening, and more and more of them seemed to come from the golden letters until all the air was full of them, and one angel came quite close to me and touched me on the shoulder where I lay—right here in my room, just think—and he said: 'Little president'—he called me 'little president' just as the secretary did when he wrote to me that nice letter after I wrote him about our new society and told him how young I was—'Dear little president,' he said, 'you are one of us now, for we are Christian Endeavorers too, though our work is different from yours, but it is going on all the time. We are the "ministering spirits." God our

Father loves your society and will bless it.' And then I felt it all so wonderful! I was just here in my bed, you know, and my head was aching so hard just a minute before, and there was the great piece of sky that I see from the window every day, and the hills at the foot of it, and there in the center of it the beautiful great gold badge, with the air full of lights and angels from it, and the most beautiful music floating all about. I was so glad and so astonished at it all that God should have taken so much trouble to send word to me, that I almost let the angel go away without saying anything but 'Thank you' to him; but just as he turned with a lovely smile to fly back, I asked him if he would please see that something was done for a few people down here in our society who didn't love Jesus. Then he put his hand on my head and smiled again, and there was a look in his eyes that I'm sure meant yes, as he went back into the center of the light again. I could see him all the way, just as clearly as when he stood beside me, and when he reached the very center of the brightness the music got farther away again, and the angels all went back, and the Heaven's badge grew dim, and pretty soon was all covered up, and I only heard the music; and pretty soon the music was the hymn you were singing in the other room, 'God be with you till we meet again,' and your meeting was breaking up. But I wish you could have seen it, and don't you think it was wonderful?"

Later, after Franklin had taken Lois home, and come back to kiss the little brother good-night, Harley put his arm about his neck and drew his face close down to his own.

"Frank," he whispered, with his lips to the young man's ear, "you were one of those that I asked the angel about, and I wanted him to be very sure about you, because I love you so much."

The older brother finished the good-night greeting hastily, and drew away to hide his emotion, but there was a warmth in the quick grasp that he gave the little hand, that Harley knew meant that he understood and appreciated.

Now about this time there fell to the lot of that society a bit of good fortune and happiness such as they had not dreamed of. The society which had been expected to entertain the State convention in the spring was somewhat disabled, and wrote to say that they must withdraw their invitation, whereupon the State secretary and executive committee, having heard of the rapid growth of the Parkerstown Society, wrote to know if they would like to entertain the convention. Ah! Wouldn't they? Such honor was almost enough to take the breath away! The dear young president was so excited that they almost had to keep him away from the next Sunday's meeting. To have a real convention right there in their society, the first year, and the national secretary coming to it too, and perhaps—oh, wonderful hope!—perhaps, the dear Father Endeavor himself—for that was the hope that the State secretary held out to them.

"Oh, Lois!" he said, with his eyes shining very brightly, and his hands clasped tightly together with excitement, "this must have been part of what the angel meant when he came out of the letters in the sky and said God would bless our society. I can't go to much of the convention myself, of course, because our room will not be large enough, and the meetings will have to be held in the church, but you can tell me all about them as you do Sundays about the service, and we shall have some real delegates in the house to talk to, for mother said so; she said we could have four. Just think, and that perhaps they would be willing if the secretary and Father Endeavor came, that they would stop here on account of my not being able to go out to hear them. Do you think others would mind and think me very greedy? Because I should want to have a little of them you know, and then perhaps they would have just one meeting here in our room. The consecration meeting would be so grand, or a morning prayer meeting; I should so like it!"

It was decided that the convention should come, and there was much looking forward to it, and the meetings grew in interest and in spirituality.

"Oh," said Harley one afternoon at the close of the meeting, "I wish that every day was Sunday! If only our meetings could last longer. I did not want it to be out to-day at all."

But the mother looked anxiously at her boy, and was thankful in her heart that every day was not filled with excitement for him. It was getting more and more apparent to the ones who were watching him closely, that Harley was not to stay with them much longer. They had questioned whether the meetings which were so dear to him were not, after all, doing him harm, and perhaps ought to be stopped; but the wise doctor shook his head sadly, and said:

"No; if he is careful not to get too excited,

it can do but little harm. The disease will have its way, do what we will. The end is not far off, I fear, but I do not think that will hasten it. The boy is getting to be such a power in this community that I do not see how we can do without him." And he went slowly from the room with bent head, while the mother covered her face with her hands, and sat down to silent grief.

Spring was coming. The convention time was near at hand, when the summons came to the little president to leave his society. He had been very ill for a whole week. On Sunday the society had met in the south room but to pray through the whole hour. Lois and Franklin were near Harley constantly. He could not bear to have them out of his sight.

It was the balmiest morning the spring had given them yet. The birds were trying some summer carols, and the breeze brought a few stray notes in at the open window. But to those in the room the notes had a sad sound, that told of some great change about to come. The whole family were gathered about Harley's bed, for he had passed through a night of suffering, and Dr. Fremont had told them he could not last much longer. He suddenly opened his eyes and looked up as Lois softly entered the room, her arms full of the splendid white lilies he loved so much.

"Lois," he said, smiling, and putting out his thin little hand to touch the flowers, "I don't think I can stay to the convention here after all. I'm sorry not to see the secretary and Father Endeavor, and all the delegates, but I think I can't stay. I saw the badge in the sky again this morning; it was brighter than before, and the angel came and spoke to me, and he said there was a convention in Heaven now, and they wanted me for a delegate from Parkerstown, and I'm to stay, Lois. The delegates to that convention all stay, and it's to get ready for the great convention when you're all coming—the angel told me so. And I don't feel so bad about not seeing Father Endeavor and the secretary now, for they will come to the great convention pretty soon. It's only a little while, and I'm to see Jesus, you know. Besides, I shall be able to do real work up there, and not have to lie on a bed, as I do here. He promised me. He asked me whom I would leave to do my work for me if I went, and I told him I didn't think it mattered about that, that I was only a little invalid boy down here, and that I had been doing pieces of other people's work. But he said no; I had a work of my own, and that I must give it to some one else to do. I thought of you,

Lois, but I decided that you had enough of your own work to do, so I told him that I thought my brother Franklin would do it. You will, won't you Franklin? You'll have to give yourself to Jesus, you know, and then you can do it, and you didn't have a work of your own. So he said it would be all right. You will, won't you, Franklin?"

The strong young man bowed his head on the pillow beside his brother and grasped the dear little hand held out so pleadingly, promising to take the commission. Harley's other worn white hand went feebly up to his breast, where was fastened the beloved gold pin, which he wore night and day. He took it off, and tried to fasten it in Franklin's coat, but was too weak to do so.

"Put it on and keep it. The angel told me I wouldn't need it up there, because he would introduce me as the delegate from Parkerstown, and they would know all about me. I think I know what makes that pin shine so now; it's the light from the letters in Heaven, that catches all the pins in the earth. You'll take good care of it, Franklin, won't you? and you'll take my place and work with Lois. She'll show you how. I wish you would find a verse to read for me at the next consecration meeting. I'm sorry not to be there, and oh! if you would say

something for me at the consecration meeting
of the convention I should like it, because I
can't be there, you know; and if they should
call my name I should like some answer to be
made to it. Good-by, mother and father, I must
go now, the light is coming in the sky again,
and the angel will be here for me. I thought I
caught a glimpse of the throne when the
letters opened the last time, and maybe I shall
see Jesus right away. Good-by."

And the little president of one winter passed
into the "Great Convention which never
breaks up," and to the "Sabbath which has no
end," having accomplished more for Christ
during his short winter than many of us do in
a life-time.

> *Weep if we may—bend low as ye pray!*
> *What does it mean?*
> *Listen! God fashioned a house. He said:*
> *"Build it with care."*
> *Then softly laid the soul . . .*
> *To dwell in there.*
>
> *And always he watched it—guarded it so,*
> *Both day and night;*
> *The wee soul grew as your lilies do,*
> *Splendid and white.*

It grew, I say, as your lilies grow,
Tender and tall;
Till God smiled, "Now the house is too low
For the child, and small."

And gently he shut the shutters one night,
And closed the door;
"More room and more light to walk upright
On a Father's floor."

Introductory Note

MY DEAR MR. LOTHROP:—

I have read Miss Livingston's little idyl with much pleasure. I cannot but think that if the older and more sedate members of the Chautauquan circles will read it, they will find that there are grains of profit in it; hidden grains, perhaps, but none the worse for being hidden at the first, if they only discover them. Miss Livingston has herself evidently understood the spirit of the movement in which the Chautauquan reading circles are engaged. That is more than can be said of everybody who expresses an opinion upon them. It is because she expresses no opinion, but rather tells, very simply, the story of the working out of the plan, that I am glad you are going to publish her little poem: for poem it is, excepting that it is not in verse or in rhyme. Believe me,

> *Very truly yours,*
> *EDWARD EVERETT HALE.*

A Chautauqua Idyl

DOWN in a rocky pasture, on the edge of a wood, ran a little brook, tinkle, tinkle, over the bright pebbles of its bed. Close to the water's edge grew delicate ferns, and higher up the mossy bank nestled violets, blue and white and yellow.

Later in the fall the rocky pasture would glow with golden-rod and brilliant sumach, and ripe milk-weed pods would burst and fill the golden autumn sunshine with fleecy clouds. But now the nodding buttercups and smiling daisies held sway, with here and there a tall mullein standing sentinel.

It was a lovely place: off in the distance one could see the shimmering lake, to whose loving embrace the brook was forever hastening, framed by beautiful wooded hills, with a hazy purple mountain back of all.

But the day was not lovely. The clouds came down to the earth as near as they dared, scowling ominously. It was clear they had been drinking deeply. A sticky, misty rain filled the air, and the earth looked sad, very sad.

The violets had put on their gossamers and drawn the hoods up over their heads, the ferns looked sadly drabbled, and the buttercups and daisies on the opposite bank, didn't even lean across to speak to their neighbors, but drew their yellow caps and white bonnets further over their faces, drooped their heads and wished for the rain to be over. The wild roses that grew on a bush near the bank hid under their leaves. The ferns went to sleep; even the trees leaned disconsolately over the brook and wished for the long, rainy afternoon to be over, while little tired wet birds in their branches never stirred, nor even spoke to each other, but stood hour after hour on one foot, with their shoulders hunched up, and one eye shut.

At last a little white violet broke the damp stillness.

"Oh dear!" she sighed, "this is so tiresome, I wish we could do something nice. Won't some one please talk a little?"

No one spoke, and some of the older ferns even scowled at her, but little violet was not to be put down. She turned her hooded face on a tall pink bachelor button growing by her side.

This same pink button was a new-comer among them. He had been brought, a little brown seed, by a fat robin, early in the spring, and dropped down close by this sweet violet.

"Mr. Button," she said, "you have been a great traveller. Won't you tell us some of your experiences?"

"Yes, yes; tell, tell, tell," babbled the brook.

The warm wind clapped him on the shoulder, and shook him gently, crying,—"Tell them, old fellow, and I'll fan them a bit while you do it."

"Tell, tell," chirped the birds overhead.

"Oh yes!" chorused the buttercups and daisies.

The little birds opened one eye and perked their heads in a listening attitude, and all the violets put their gossamer hoods behind their ears so that they might hear better.

"Well, I might tell you about Chautauqua," said pink bachelor thoughtfully.

"And what is Chautauqua?" questioned a saucy little fish who had stopped on his way to the lake to listen.

"Chautauqua is a place, my young friend, a beautiful place, where I spent last summer with my family," said the bachelor in a very patronizing tone.

"Oh! you don't say so," said the naughty little fish with a grimace, and sped on his way to the lake, to laugh with all the other fishes at the queer new word.

"Go on, go on, go on," sang the brook.

"We lived in a garden by a house just outside the gates," began Bachelor.

"What gates?" interrupted the eager daisies.

"Why, the gates of the grounds."

"What grounds?"

"Why, the grounds of Chautauqua."

"But who is Chautauqua?" asked the puzzled violets.

"Don't you know? Chautauqua is a beautiful place in the woods, shut in from the world by a high fence all around it, with locked gates. It is on the shore of a lovely lake. Many people come there every year, and they have meetings, and they sing beautiful songs about birds and flowers and sky and water and God and angels and dear little babies and stars. Men come there from all over this world, and stand up and talk high, grand thoughts, and the people listen and wave their handkerchiefs till it looks like an orchard full of cherry trees in blossom.

"They have lovely singers—ladies who sing

alone as sweet as birds, and they have great grand choruses of song besides, by hundreds of voices. And they have instruments to play on,—organs and pianos, and violins and harps."

"How beautiful," murmured the flowers.

"Tell us more," said the brook; "tell us more, more, more,—tell, tell, tell!"

"More, more," said the wind.

"It lasts all summer, so the people who can't come at one time will come at another, though my cousin said she thought that one day all the people in the world came at once. There must have been something very grand to bring so many that day. There were not enough rooms for visitors to sleep in, and Chautauqua is a large place, the largest I was ever in. Yes," Bachelor said reflectively, "I think all the world must have been there."

The little white violet looked up.

"There was one day last summer when no one came through the pasture, and no one went by on the road, and all day long we saw not one person. It must have been that day, and they were all gone to Chautauqua," she said softly.

"I shouldn't wonder at all," said Bachelor.

Then they all looked sober and still. They were thinking. The idea that all the people in the world had come together for a day was very great to them.

At last one spoke:

"How nice it would be if all the flowers in the world could come together for a day," said the little violet.

"And all the birds," chirped a sparrow.

"And all the brooks and lakes and ocean," laughed the brook.

"And all the trees," sighed the tall elm.

"Oh! and all the winds. We could make as beautiful music as ever any organ or piano made."

"But what is it all for?" asked a bright-eyed daisy.

"To teach the people all about the things that the great God has made, and show them how to live to please Him, and how to please Him in the best way," promptly answered Bachelor.

"There is a great good man at the head of it, and I heard a lady say that God Himself sent him there to take care of Chautauqua for Him, for it is all made to praise God. They have schools,—everybody studies, but it is all about God that they learn,—about the things He made, or how to praise Him better, and all the talking,—they call it lecturing,—is to help men to praise and love God more. They have three beautiful mottoes:

"'We study the word and works of God.' 'Let us keep our Heavenly Father in our midst,' and, 'Never be discouraged.'"

"Wonderful, wonderful, wonderful," said the old forest tree.

"It is just what we need," piped one of the birds. "We don't praise God half enough. Here we've been sitting and sulking all the afternoon because it is raining, and never one thankful chirp have we given for all the yesterdays and yesterdays when it hasn't rained. We need a Chautauqua. I declare, I'm ashamed!" And he poured forth such a glad, thankful song of praise as thrilled the old forest trees through and through and most effectually waked the napping ferns.

"Yes," said the listening daisies, when the song was done and the bird had stopped to rest his throat, "we do need a Chautauqua."

"Let's have a Chautauqua!" cried the brook.

"But how could we," said the wise-eyed violet, "when we know so little about it?"

"I will tell you all I know," said Bachelor graciously. "You see we lived just outside the gates, and people used often to come and buy my brothers and sisters. Once a young man came and bought a very large bunch of them and took them to a young lady in a white dress, and she wore them everywhere for three or four days—you know our family is a very long-lived one, and we are something like the camel, in that we can go a long time without a drink of water—well, she kept them carefully and took them everywhere she went, and they saw and heard a great many new things. One evening this young lady sat in a big place full of people, and an old lady sitting behind her said to another lady, 'Just see those pink bachelor buttons! My mother used to have some just like them growing in her garden, years and years ago, and I haven't seen any since.' The young lady heard her, turned around and gave her a whole handful of my brothers and sisters. After the meeting was out, the old lady carried them away with her, but one slipped out of her hand and fell on the walk, and some one came along in the darkness and crushed her. Quite early the next morning our neighbor, Mr. Robin, going to the market for a worm for breakfast, saw her lying in this sad state, and with great difficulty brought her home to us. She lived only a day or two longer, but long enough to tell us many of her experiences.

"After she had faded and gone, our friend

Robin went every day to hear and see what was going on inside the great gates, and every night when the bells were ringing"—

"What bells?" interrupted an impolite buttercup.

"The night bells for the people to go to sleep by. They rang beautiful music on bells by the water to put the people to sleep, and in the morning to wake them, and they had bells to call them to the big place to praise God, and hear the lectures and singing."

"Beautiful, beautiful," murmured the brook.

"And every night," proceeded the bachelor, "when the bells were ringing we would wake up and Robin would tell us all about the day inside the gates. Of course I can't remember all, but I will tell you all I know."

"Perhaps I can help you a little," spoke out an old fish who had come up the stream unobserved some time before. "I lived in Lake Chautauqua myself for some years until my daughter sent for me to come and live with her in yonder lake."

They all looked at the old fish with great veneration, and thanked him kindly.

"Well, how shall we begin?" said an impatient daisy.

"I should think the first thing to be done is to make a motion that we have a Chautauqua," Bachelor said.

Then rose up a tall old fern. "I make a motion to that effect."

"I second it," chirped a sparrow.

"All in favor of the motion say 'aye,'" said Bachelor, in a deep, important voice.

And then arose such a chorus of "aye's" as never was heard before in that grove. The wind blew it, the brook gurgled it, the great forest trees waved it, all the little flowers filled the air with their perfumed voices, the far-off lake murmured its assent, the purple mountain nodded its weary old head, the sun shot triumphantly through the dark clouds, and all God's works seemed joining in the "aye, aye, aye" that echoed from hillside to wood.

"A unanimous vote, I think," said Bachelor, after the excitement had somewhat subsided.

"The next question is, When shall we have it?"

"Oh! right away, of course," nodded a buttercup. "See! the sun has come out to help us."

"But," objected white Violet, "we can't. We must invite all the flowers and birds and brooks and trees all over the world, and they will have to get ready. It will take the flowers the rest of this summer and all of next winter to get their dresses made and packed in their brown travelling seed trunks. I'm sure it would me if I were to go away from here for the summer, and it is late in the season already. We couldn't get word to them all in time."

"Yes," said the fish, "and there are the travelling expenses to be arranged for such a large company. We should have to secure reduced rates. They always do on Chautauqua Lake."

"Oh! as to that," said the wind, "I and the birds would do the transportation free of charge, and the brook would do all it could, I'm sure."

"Of course, of course," babbled the brook.

"That is very kind of you indeed," said Bachelor. "But I should think that the earliest possible beginning that we could hope to have would be next spring."

After much impatient arguing on the part of the buttercups and daisies, it was finally agreed that the first meeting of their Chautauqua should be held the following spring.

"It must last all summer," they said, "because some of us can come early and some late. There is the golden-rod now, it never can come till late in the fall."

"Of course, of course; certainly, certainly," chattered the brook.

"What comes next?" softly asked the wild rose.

"The next thing to do is to appoint a committee to make out the programme," remarked the fish.

"Committee! Who is that?" cried a butterfly.

"Programme! what's programme?" chirped a sparrow.

"Oh dear! we need a dictionary," sighed the roses.

"What's a dictionary?" asked a little upstart of a fern.

"Silence!" sternly commanded Bachelor. "Will Miss Rose kindly explain the meaning of dictionary, after which Mr. Fish will proceed to tell us about programme and committee."

Little Rose blushed all over her pretty face, and after thinking a moment, replied,—

"A dictionary is a book that tells what all words mean."

"Oh!" sighed the wind, "we must have a dictionary."

Mr. Fish having made a dash up stream after a fly, now resumed his sedate manner and spoke:

"My friends, a programme says what we will have every day, and a committee are the ones who make it."

"Then let's all be committee," said the buttercup.

"That's a very good plan," said Bachelor. "Now, what shall we have? They always have a prayer meeting first at Chautauqua."

"We can all pray," said the elm. "Let us have a prayer meeting first every morning to thank the dear God for the new day, and let the rising sun be the leader."

"That is good," said the flowers, and bright rays of light, the sun's little children, kissed them tenderly.

"What is next?"

"They have a large choir, and every morning after the prayer meeting they meet and practise with the great organ and piano and band."

"We will be the singers," chorused the birds.

"I will tinkle, tinkle, like a piano." sang the brook, "tinkle, tinkle, tinkle,—"

"I will play the band, for I have very many instruments at my command, and my friend the thunder will play the organ, while you, dear old trees, shall be my violins and harps, and every morning we will practise," said the wind.

"What do they have next at Chautauqua?" asked a pert blackbird.

"Lectures," said the fish.

"What are lectures?"

"Talks about things."

"What things?"

"Oh! evolution and literature and theology and philosophy and art and poetry and science, and a great many other things."

The high-sounding words rolled out from that fish's mouth as if he actually thought he understood them.

Silence reigned for a few minutes, deep and intense, at last broken by the white violet:

"We never could have all those, for we don't know anything about them. And who could talk about such things? None of us."

Silence again. They were all thinking earnestly.

"I don't believe it. Not one word." chattered a saucy squirrel. "That's a fish story. As if *you* could get on dry land and go to lectures."

"Oh! very well, you needn't believe it if you don't want to," answered the fish in a hurt tone, "but I heard a man on board the steamer read the programme, and those are the very words he read."

"If we only had a dictionary," again sighed the rose.

"Dictionary, dictionary, dic, dic, dictionary," murmured the brook, thoughtfully.

"A dictionary is absolutely necessary before we can proceed any further," said the south wind. "And as I am obliged to travel to New York this evening, I will search everywhere, and if possible bring one back with me. Anything can be had in New York. It is getting late, and I think we had better adjourn to meet again to-morrow. I hope to be able to return by two o'clock. In the meantime, let us all think deeply of what we have heard, and if any one can see a way out of our difficulty, let him tell us then."

The sunbeams kissed the flowers goodnight, the forest trees waved farewell to the good wind, the brook called, "Good-night! sweet dreams till to-morrow, to-morrow, to-morrow," and all the air was soft with bird vespers.

Into the bright sunshine of the next afternoon came the winds and the eager birds to the place on the bank where the violets grew.

The daisies leaned far over the bank to listen.

The south wind came bringing two or three torn sheets of an old dictionary.

"It is all I could find, and I've had hard work to get this," said he. "I went in at a window where lay an open dictionary.—I had no idea that a dictionary was such a very large book.—It was an old one, so I had no trouble in tearing out these few leaves, as the paper was so tender. I took them out of the window and hid them in a safe place and went back for more, but just as I was turning the leaves over to find evolution, some one came up and shut the window, and I had to crawl out through the cracks. Well, I have all the 'P's' and some of the 'T's'; we can find theology and poetry."

"Philosophy, too," said wise Violet.

"My dear, that is spelled with an 'f,'" said the kind old wind patronizingly.

"Oh no! I am sure you are mistaken. It is 'p-h-i-l'; look and see if I am not right."

The wind slowly turned over the leaves of his meagre dictionary, and, sure enough, there it was,—"p-h-i-l-o-s-o-p-h-y."

"Is it there? What does it say?" questioned the eager flowers.

"Philosophy, the love of, or search after, wisdom," slowly read the wind.

"Oh!" said the flowers, "is that all it is? Why, we know philosophy."

"I think the forest trees could lecture on philosophy," said the wind.

"Yes, yes, yes," they all cried. "The forest trees, for they are very old and have had longer to search for wisdom than we."

"Very well; three lectures a week on philosophy, by the old forest trees; write it down, please," cried Bachelor.

The secretary, a scarlet-headed woodpecker, carefully carved it on the trunk of an old tree, and I think you can still find the minutes of that day written in lines of beauty all over the tree.

"Theology is the next word," announced the wind, and again turned over the leaves of their precious dictionary.

"The science of God," he read. "Science, what is science?" If we only had the 's's'!"

"I know what it is," chirped a bird. "I hopped into the schoolhouse this morning, and a book was open on the desk, and no one was there, so I hopped up and took a look to see if there was anything in it to help us. The first words my eye fell on were these,—'science is knowledge.' And I didn't wait for any more, but flew away to sit in a tree and say it over so that I wouldn't forget it. Going back a little later to see if I could get any more words, I found the schoolhouse full of dreadful boys. As I flew away again, this little piece of paper blew out of the window, and I brought it, thinking it might be helpful."

As he finished speaking, he deposited a small fragment of a definition spelling-book at the foot of the elm tree, and flew up into the branches again, for he was a bashful bird, and this was a very long speech for him to make before so many.

"Good, good, good," cried all the committee.

"To go back to theology," said the wind. "It is the science of God. Science is knowledge, therefore theology is knowledge of God. That is a very great thing. Who is able to lecture on the knowledge of God?"

Silence all. No one dared to volunteer. None felt worthy to do so great a thing.

Out spoke a shy little wren. "Last night I slept in a notch close over a church window, and the window was open and there was a meeting of the people there and the minister read out of the Bible these words: 'The heav-

ens declare the glory of God, and the firmament sheweth his handiwork.'"

She paused a moment to gather courage,
and then said, "Why couldn't the heavens
teach theology?"

"Bless your heart, little wren, that is the very
thing," cried the blustering north wind. And
all the flowers cried,—"The heavens shall
teach theology!"

The sky bowed its assent and said, "I will do
my best to perform the wonderful work en-
trusted to me."

And the happy brook murmured, "Glory,
glory, glory! the glory of God."

"Now we will see what this bit of paper has
for us," said the wind as he picked up the
paper at the foot of the elm.

"Ah! What have we here? Evolution! Just
what we want: 'evolution, the act of unfolding
or unrolling.'"

He stopped with a thoughtful look.

"Yes, I see. As the young leaves and flowers
unfold. The plants must take full charge of this
department, I think. I remember once turning
over the leaves of a fat, dark-gray book, with
gilt letters on its back. It lay on a minister's
window-seat, and it looked interesting, so I
read a few minutes while the minister was out

and not using it, and among other things that I read was this, and it stayed with me ever since: 'A lily grows mysteriously. Shaped into beauty by secret and invisible fingers, the flower develops, we know not how. Every day the thing is done: it is God.' You see, my dear," addressing himself to a pure white lily that had only that morning unfolded its delicate petals to the sun, "you see a great many don't understand how it is done. You need to tell how God has made you able to unfold."

"Yes, we will, we can," they all cried.

"The flowers will speak on Evolution," wrote down Woodpecker.

"There are three more words spoken by our friend Fish, still unexplained,—literature,—"

"I know what literature means, Mr. Wind, it is books," announced a bright butterfly who had just arrived on the scene.

"Are you sure?" questioned the fish doubtfully.

"Yes; of course I am. I went with a big pinch-bug one day into a great room full of books, and he said, when he saw the shelves and shelves full of them, 'My! what a lot of literature!'"

The committee looked convinced, but now came the question of books,—Where should they get them? How could they lecture on books, when they knew nothing about them?

"We must just send word around to all the flowers and birds and trees and everything, to see who can lecture on books, and we must all keep our eyes and ears open," said a buttercup bud.

"We shall have to lay that on the table for the present," said the wind.

"But we haven't any table," chattered a squirrel.

"A well brought-up squirrel should know better than to interrupt. We shall have to put this aside, then, until we can learn more about it. In the meantime, let us proceed with the next word on the list, poetry."

"I know," said the brook. "A bit of paper lay upon my bank, miles and miles away from here, too high up for me to reach, but I could read it. It said, 'For poetry is the blossom and the fragrance of all human knowledge.' And I have said it over and over all the way here."

"Ah! the flowers shall give us poetry," said the good old wind.

Bachelor bowed his head and said, "We will try."

"Try, try, try," chattered the brook.

"Art is next, I believe," said Bachelor.

"Yes, art," said a squirrel.

"Art is making pictures,"said the moss.

"Then the sunset must paint them, for there are no pictures made like those of the sunset," said the wind.

The sun hastened to mix his paint, and in answer to the request that he would be professor of art, painted one of the most glorious sunset scenes that mortal eye has ever looked upon. Rapidly he dashed on the color, delicate greens and blues blending with the sea-shell pink, and glowing with deep crimson and gold, till the assembled committee fairly held their breaths with delight. The crimson and gold and purple in the west were beginning to fade and mix with soft greys and tender yellows, before the committee thought of returning to their work.

"What a lot of time we have wasted," said the oldest squirrel; "to-morrow is Sunday, and of course we can't work then, and now it is time to go home."

"Not wasted, dear squirrel," said White Violet, "not wasted when we were looking at God's beautiful sunset."

Bachelor looked down at her in all her sweetness and purity, and some of the flowers say that later when he went to bid her good-night—under the shadow of a fern—he kissed her.

"To-morrow being Sunday reminds me that we have not made any arrangements for our Sunday sermons. They always have great sermons at Chautauqua, and I have often heard the passengers on the steamer scolding because the boats did not run on Sunday, for they said the great men always kept their best thoughts for sermons." This from the fish.

They all paused. "We can't any of us preach sermons, what shall we do?" questioned a fern.

"I'm sure I don't know; we might each of us go to church and listen to a sermon and preach it over again," said a thoughtful bird.

"But we couldn't remember it all, and by next summer we would have forgotten it entirely," said one more cautious.

"Well, we must go," said the wind. "Monday we will consider these subjects. To-morrow is God's day, and we must go immediately, for it is getting dark."

And so they all rested on the Sabbath day, and praised the great God, and never a wee violet, nor even a chattering chipmunk, allowed his thoughts to wander off to the great programme for the next summer, but gave their thoughts to holy things.

The busy Monday's work was all done up, and the committee gathered again, waiting for the work to go on, when there came flying in great haste, a little bluebird, and, breathless, stopped on a branch to rest a moment ere he tried to speak.

"What is the matter?" they all cried.

"Were you afraid you would be late? You ought not to risk your health; it is not good to get so out of breath," said a motherly old robin.

"Oh! I have such good news to tell you," cried the little bird as soon as he could speak. "I sat on a bough this morning, close to a window where sat an old lady, who was reading aloud to a sick man, so I stopped to listen. These are the words she read,—'Sermons in stones, books in running brooks.' I didn't hear any more, but came right away to study that. I was so glad I had found something to help us. Two things in one."

They all looked very much amazed.

"Why, we didn't think we could do anything!" cried the stones, "and here we can do one of the best things there is to be done. Thank the dear God for that. We will preach sermons full of God and his works, for we have seen a great many ages, and their story is locked up in us."

"And the brook shall tell us of books," said the old wind. "There is good in everything, and we shall try not to feel discouraged the next time we are in a difficulty."

"Books in running brooks," said the brook. "Books, books, books. And I too can praise Him."

"This morning," said a sober-looking bird, "a small girl just under my nest in the orchard, was saying something over and over to herself, and I listened; and these were the words that she said:

> The ocean looketh up to heaven as 'twere a living thing,
> The homage of its waves is given in ceaseless worshipping.
> They kneel upon the sloping sand, as bends thehuman knee,
> A beautiful and tireless band, the priesthood of the sea,
> They pour the glittering treasures out which in the deep have birth,
> And chant their awful hymns about the watching-hills of earth.

"If the ocean is so good and grand as that he ought to do something at our Chautauqua.

Couldn't he? God must love him very much, he worships him so much."

"Yes," said the elm tree. "I have heard that a great man once said, 'God, God, God walks on thy watery rim.'"

"Wonderful, glorious," murmured the flowers.

"They tell stories at Chautauqua—pretty stories about things and people; and I have heard that Ocean has a wonderful story. We might send word to ask if he will tell it," suggested Bachelor.

"I fear he cannot leave home," said the wind, "but we might try him."

So it was agreed that the woodpecker should write a beautiful letter, earnestly inviting him to take part in the grand new movement for the coming summer. The brook agreed to carry the daintily-carved missive to the lake, and the lake to the river, and the river would carry it to the sea.

Bachelor spoke next: "They have a School of Languages at Chautauqua, could we have one?"

"I have thought of that," said the fish, "but who could teach it?"

"That is the trouble," said Bachelor, slowly shaking his head.

"I know," said a little bird. "I went to church last night and heard the Bible read, and it said, 'Day unto day uttereth speech, and night unto night sheweth knowledge. There is no speech nor language where their voice is not heard.' I think the day and the night could teach the School of Languages."

"The day and the night, the day and the night," said the brook.

"Yes," said the oldest tree of all, "the day and the night know all languages."

"We must have a Missionary Day and a Temperance Day," said the wise old fish.

"What is a Temperance Day?" asked a young squirrel, who was not yet very well acquainted with the questions of the day.

"My dear," said his mother, "there are some bad people in the world who make vile stuff and give it to people to drink, and it makes them sick and cross; then they do not please God, and there are some good people who are trying to keep the bad people from making it, and the others from drinking it; they are called Temperance."

"Oh!" said the squirrel, "but why do the folks drink it? I should think they'd know better."

"So should I, but they don't. Why, my dear, I must tell you of something that happened to me once. I lived in a tree at a summer resort, that year, and just under my bough was a window; a young man roomed there for a few days, and every morning he would come to the window with a black bottle in his hand, and pour out some dark stuff and mix sugar and water with it, and drink it as if he thought it was very good. I watched him for several mornings, and one morning the bell rang while he was drinking, and he left the glass on the window-sill, and went to breakfast. I hopped down to see what it was, and it smelled good, so I tasted it. I liked the taste pretty well, so I drank all there was left. Then I started home, but, will you believe it? I could not walk straight, and very soon I could hardly stand up. I tried to climb up a tree, but fell off the first bough, and there I lay for a long, long time. When I awoke I had such a terrible pain in my head! All that day I suffered, and didn't get over my bad feelings for several days. I tell this as a warning to you, that you may never be tempted to touch anything to drink but water, my dear."

"You must tell that story, Mrs. Squirrel," said Bachelor. "And we will call it a story of intemperance, by one of its victims."

"I will, with all my heart, if it will do any one any good," she responded.

"Yes, we must have a Temperance Day and all make a speech on drinking cold water," said the fish.

"And dew," said the violet.

"I have always drunk water, and never anything else, and I think one could scarcely find an older or a healthier tree than I am," said the elm.

"That is true," said the fish.

"Cold water, cold water, cold water," babbled the brook.

"Yes, we can all speak on Temperance Day; we will have a great platform meeting. That is what they call it at Chautauqua when a great many speak about one thing. I heard a man telling his little girl about it on the boat," said the fish.

And the woodpecker wrote it down.

"What was that other you said?" asked a sharp little chipmunk.

"Missionary Day," said the fish.

"And what is that?"

"Why, there are home missions and foreign missions," said the fish. "And they talk about them both. I think they have a day for each, or maybe two or three. Missions are doing good to some one, but I don't exactly see the difference between home and foreign missions."

"Why, that is plain to me," said Bachelor. "Home missions is when some one does something kind to you, and foreign missions is when you do something kind to some one else."

"Of course; why didn't I think of that before?" said the fish.

"One day last year I was very hungry," said a robin, "very hungry and cold. I had come on too early in the season. There came a cold snap, and the ground was frozen. I could find nothing at all to eat. I was almost frozen myself, and had begun to fear that my friends would come on to find me starved to death instead of getting ready for them as expected. But a little girl saw me and threw some crumbs out of the window. I went and ate them, and every day as long as the cold weather lasted she threw me crumbs—such good ones too—some of them cake; and she gave me silk ravelings to make my nest of. I think that was a home mission, don't you?"

"Yes, my dear, it was," said Bachelor.

"You might tell that as one thing," said the wind.

"I will," said Birdie.

Said a daisy, "When I was very thirsty, one

day, and the clouds sent down no good rain, the dear brook jumped up high here, and splashed on me so I could drink, and I think that was a home mission."

"Yes, yes," said the elm, "it was."

"I know a story I could tell," said the ferns.

"And I," said the elm; "one of many years ago, when I was but a little twig."

"I know a home mission story too," said White Violet.

"And I," said the brook. "Once I was almost all dried up and could hardly reach the lake, and a dear lovely spring burst up and helped me along until the dry season was over."

"And I, and I," chorused a thousand voices.

"But what about foreign missions?" said the fish.

"I sang a beautiful song to a sad old lady in a window, this morning," said a mocking-bird.

"That's foreign missions," said the chipmunk.

"Some naughty boys hid another boy's hat yesterday, and I found it for him and blew it to his feet," said the wind.

"I sent a bunch of buds to a sick girl, this morning," said the rose-bush with a blush.

"I think we shall have no lack of foreign missions," remarked Bachelor.

"But what can *we* do?" asked an old gray squirrel. "We can't preach, nor teach. We can run errands and carry messages, but that isn't much."

"You might be on the commissary department," said the wind.

"What's that?" they all asked.

"Things to eat. We shall need a great many, and you could all lay in a stock of nuts, enough to last all summer, for a great many."

"Why, surely!" they cried, and all that fall such a hurrying and scurrying from bough to bough there was as never was seen before. They worked very hard, storing up nuts, and the people came near not getting any at all.

It must have been about a week from the time they sent their letter to Old Ocean, that one afternoon as they were assembled, waiting for the decision of a certain little committee, which had been sent over behind a stone to decide who should be the leader of the choir, that up the stream came a weary little fish.

He was unlike any fish that had ever been seen in that brook, and caused a great deal of remark among the flowers before he was within hearing distance.

He came wearily, as though he had travelled

a long distance, but as he drew nearer, the old fish exclaimed, "There comes a salt-water fish! perhaps he has a message from the ocean."

Then the little company were all attention.

Nearer and nearer he came, and stopped before the old fish with a low bow, inquiring whether this was the Chautauqua Committee.

On being told that it was, he laid a bit of delicate sea-weed, a pearly shell, and a beautiful stem of coral upon the bank, and said: "I have a message from Old Ocean for you. He sends you greetings and many good wishes for the success of your plan, and regrets deeply that he cannot be with you next summer; but he is old, very old, and he has so much to do that he cannot leave even for a day or two. If he should, the world would be upside down. There would be no rain in the brooks, the lakes would dry up, and the crops and the people all would die."

"Oh dear! and we should die too," said the flowers.

"Yes, you would die, too," said the salt-water fish.

"He has a great many other things besides to take care of; there are the great ships to carry from shore to shore, and there is the telegraph,—"

"What is telegraph?" interrupted that saucy little squirrel who had no regard even for a stranger's presence.

"Telegraph is a big rope that people send letters to their friends on. It is under the water in the ocean, and the letters travel so fast that we have never yet been able to see them, though we have watched night and day."

"Wonderful, strange," they all murmured.

"Old Ocean says," proceeded the messenger, "that he cannot give you all of his story, as it would be too long, but that he sends some of it written on this shell, and in this coral and in this bit of sea-weed. In the shell is a drop of pure salt water that if carefully examined will tell you many more wonderful things."

They all thanked the fish kindly for coming so far to bring them these treasures, and begged him to stay and rest, but he declined, saying he had a family at home and must hasten, so he turned to go.

"Stay!" cried Bachelor. "Wouldn't you be willing to come next summer and give us a lecture on the telegraph?"

The fish laughed.

"Bless you!" said he, "I couldn't do that. I don't know enough about it myself. Ask the lightning. He is the head manager, and will

give you all the lectures you want. Good-by!
the sun is getting low, and I must be off." And
he sped away, leaving the woodpecker writing
down "telegraph" and "lightning" on one
corner of his memoranda.

And now the committee returned, having
decided, by unanimous vote, that the mocking-
bird should be the leader of the choir, as he
could sing any part, and so help along the weak
ones whenever he could see the need of it.

There was a pause after the committee had
been told all that had happened during their
absence, broken at last by Bachelor.

"I've been thinking," said he, "that it might
be as well for us to have a reply to Ingersoll."

"What is that?" they asked, for they were
getting used to strange things, and did not
seem so surprised at the new word.

"Ingersoll is a man that says there is no God,
and he has written a great many things to
prove it," said Bachelor gravely.

The other poor little flowers were too
much shocked to say anything, and they all
looked at one another dumbly.

"Is he blind?" asked a bird.

"He must know better," asserted a fern.
"No one could possibly believe such a thing."

"I don't know whether he is blind, but I think not," said Bachelor. "They say he has made a great many other people believe as he does because he talks so beautifully."

"How dreadful!" said the flowers, in a sad voice.

"They had a man at Chautauqua who answered all he said and proved that it was untrue, but every one did not hear him. I think we ought to have a day to answer Ingersoll," again said Bachelor.

"Yes, we must," said the north wind; "and we will all prove there *is* a God. No one could have made me but God." And he blew and blew until the flowers crouched down almost afraid at his fierceness.

When all was quiet again, out hopped a dignified-looking bird. "My friends," said he, "my wife and I went to church last night, and they sang a beautiful hymn that has long been one of my favorites. I told my wife to listen hard, and this morning, with my help, she was able to sing it. I think it would help on this subject if we were to sing it for you now."

"Sing, sing, sing," said the brook.

The meek little wife at her husband's word stepped out, and together they sang this wonderful hymn:

The spacious firmament on high,
With all the blue ethereal sky,
The spangled heavens, a shining frame,
Their great original proclaim;
The unwearied sun, from day to day,
Does his Creator's power display,
And publishes to every land
The work of an Almighty hand.

Soon as the evening shades prevail,
The moon takes up the wondrous tale,
And nightly to the listening earth
Repeats the story of her birth:
While all the stars that round her burn,
And all the planets in their turn,
Confirm the tidings as they roll,
And spread the truth from pole to pole.

What though, in solemn silence, all
Move round the dark, terrestrial ball?
What though no real voice or sound
Amid their radiant orbs be found?
In reason's ear they all rejoice,
And utter forth a glorious voice,
Forever singing as they shine,
The hand that made us is divine.

When they had finished, the whole congregation bowed their heads.

"Yes," they said, "every day we will show forth the greatness of God who made us, and that bad man will see and hear and believe, and the people will not be led away from God any more.

"We will make that our great aim, to show forth the glory of God," they all cried together.

So the little workers planned, and sent their messengers far and wide, over land and sea, and made out their programme; and the lecturers spent days and days preparing their manuscript,—for aught I know they are at it yet.

The flowers all have received their invitations to come, and some were so eager to be off that they packed their brown seed trunks and coaxed the wind to carry them immediately, that they might be early on the spot.

Next spring when the snow is gone and the trees are putting forth their leaves, and all looks tender and beautiful, you will see the birds flying back and forth, very busy, carrying travellers and messages; the squirrels will go chattering to their store-houses to see that all is right, and to air the rooms a little; the birds will build many nests, more than they need, and you will wonder why, and will never know that they are summer nests for rent, else you might like to rent one yourself.

The wind, too, will be busy, so busy that he will hardly have time to dry your clothes that hang out among the apple blossoms.

You don't know what it all means?

Wake up quite early every morning and listen. Be patient, and one morning, just as the first pink glow of the rising sun tinges the east, you will hear a watching tree call out,—

> *The year's at the spring,*
> *And the day's at the morn;*
> *Morning's at seven;*
> *The hillside's dew pearled;*
> *The lark's on the wing;*
> *The snail's on the thorn;*
> *God's in His heaven—*
> *All's right with the world.*

And then all the lily-bells will chime out the call to prayer, the great red sun will come up and lead, and the little Chautauqua will open.

You will hear the sweet notes of praise from the bird choir, and prayers will rise from the flowers like sweet incense; you will see and hear it all, but will you remember that it is all to show forth the glory of God?

A Little Servant

HIGH in that graceful branch yonder, just under the largest maple leaf, there hides a nest. Look! Do you see the leaf rise in the wind? There! there she is, that little gray bird.

All day long the bough rocks up and down, to and fro, and all night long the stars peep through the leaves at her, and the tender moonlight sheds a golden rain around. Through all the long summer the sweet wind hovers, now singing a song of peace and love and home and joy, now lifting the green canopy overhead, to give the little mother a view of some soft cloud floating in the blue sea above. And so she sits, and broods and broods.

And when it rains? Why, it never rains at all in that sheltered nest; the leaves look out for that.

Watch! Dipping, swooping, curving, with a

flutter and a whirl, comes a wee bird, smaller than the other, and she has yellow feathers in her wings. But mother-bird's eyes are on her, and, wondering, she anxiously awaits the result of this unexpected visit.

The small visitor hops about a bit with a saucy air, eying all the time the neat and comfortable nest. Suddenly she makes a dart at a dainty bit of white cotton deftly woven into the nest, and as quickly carries away the pride and joy of the young mother-bird's heart.

It was as if when you had just finished a nice little home, with bay windows, porches and cornices, and had sat down to your sewing to enjoy it all, some one had come and quickly picked off and carried away the bay windows, porches and pretty things, leaving your house bare and forlorn.

Yes, that bit of cotton was a bay window, a porch, a cornice, and all the other beautifying things to little birdie's heart. So also thought Yellow Wings, or she would never have made such a bold attempt to steal in broad daylight.

With a cry of dismay, mother-bird darted after her, but too late, alas! Yellow Wings was fleet and wary. She knew the quickest way to get out of sight, and poor little mother-bird must come back to her dismantled home to tell her husband the sorrowful tale, and they two repair the damage as best they can. It is not the work of a day, though, for such bits of cotton are not always to be found for the looking. Poor little birds! And two watchers, standing by, saw it all.

One was— Did you ever know the little girl that lived in the pretty house, with the garden all about it? Her eyes were bits of blue left over when the sky was finished. Her hair was like curling sunbeams, and her lips all kisses and rose leaves. When she laughed 'twas like the spring wind playing amongst the violets, so low and sweet. Every one loved little Esther, and she was queen of the whole house.

There she stood on the balcony, close over the branch where madam-bird rocked all day, and saw the deed done which so darkened the cheer of the little nest. Her heart swelled with indignation that a bird could be so naughty, and her feelings took voice in a sorrowful, horrified "Oh-oo-o! Poor, poor birdie."

The other watcher stood below, leaning on his rake. He was a dark-browed young man, with a face that would have been good but for the settled look of gloom and scorn which he wore. There was a certain pride, too, such as did not match the rough gardener's suit.

All about him stretched the broad lawns, smooth as velvet, of the Carleton home, and above, the blue, blue heavens. It was a perfect day, and yet the perfection jarred on the young man. Here was all this beauty, and none of it for him. If there was a God, how could he treat him so? Where was the justice in it? He looked down with contempt at the heavy boots, and the rake which must be used, and used faithfully, for some one else, ere he could have a right to his daily bread. He hated the work he was doing, and put no pleasure in the clean-cut curves of the gravel paths on which he was working, or the well-shaped mounds he was preparing for the plants that were soon to fill them.

It was not many years since he was a boy in a home where everything was pleasant and happy; he was the pride of his father and the pet of his mother—their only child—and his every wish was gratified if possible. His father had not been rich, only comfortably off, but he had never wanted for anything. He had been a bright boy in his classes in the public school. His father had intended to educate him for a lawyer; to that end the boy was not expected to devote himself to anything but study, so he grew up with very little practical knowledge of any kind. He had not improved his opportunities for study as well as he might have done, but he did not realize that yet.

At fifteen he was in a fair way to graduate from the High School in one year more, when his education suddenly stopped. The father was killed in a railroad accident, and the little mother, not very strong at any time, never left her bed after the funeral, and in a few short days was lying beside her husband. When the poor stunned boy tried to look around him to see what he should do, they told him that he had no money, and must leave school and go to work.

The indulgent father, who had never been able to deny his son any wish, who had always granted any request of money from his wife, so that she had no idea he was not able to spare it, had not made allowance for the death angel and his possible summons to the court of heaven. The money had been spent as it was earned on little every-day comforts, and there was nothing left to the boy but hard work, for which he was not in the least prepared.

He had taken, as a matter of necessity, the place that was offered to him, but he did not know how to do the work well, and disliked it. When there came an opportunity for a change he changed, and, as is often the case when people try to better themselves, he only made himself worse off, and hated the new work more than the old. So he went from one thing to another, often out of employment, and so surly and haughty in his manner that no one cared to employ him.

He awoke one day to the fact that he was a man, twenty-four years old, with no regular employment, and, what was worse, no chance of any work whatever. He had drifted in these years far away from the old home, where he might have had friends to help him. He found himself in this strange city, having spent two weeks in fruitless hunting for something to do; in debt to the landlady of his miserable little boarding house for his board for those two weeks. What was to be done? There seemed to be nothing in the world for him to do. He had even condescended to ask one man if he didn't want his wood sawed, but had received such a sharp "No" from him that he had not the courage to ask any one else.

So when he heard Mr. Carleton inquiring for a man to do a little gardening for him, as his gardener was sick, he was glad in a sullen kind of way to accept the offered work. This was his first day at the place, and he had filled his mind with hard, bitter thoughts about himself, his lot, and the injustice of his God to have allowed it all to happen to him. You see it never occurred to this young man that he had brought part of the trouble on himself.

His mother had been a Christian, in her quiet way, always teaching him that he ought to love God, although he had not any very definite idea why. Just before she died she had said to him in a broken whisper:

"Robert, I haven't been the sort of mother I ought to have been. I haven't told you about Jesus and His love. I don't know what I should do without Him now. You must know Him, my son, and get ready to die. You will be sure to come to me in Heaven, my boy?"

He had kissed her and promised, too stunned to know what he was saying, almost; but later, when his grief had somewhat worn away, he had fallen in with companions who ridiculed his mother's God, and he had grown to think that if there was a God who loved him, he never would have let so much trouble come to him. So the promise to his mother had been set down as a foolish one, made to quiet a dying woman, and the boy grew into manhood trying to make himself believe that he never expected to see his father and mother again.

So with his mind full of gloomy thoughts he worked, looked across the lawn and saw the beauty, but took none of it into his soul. As he heard the flutter and twitter above his head he looked up and saw the little robber bird in the act of stealing the coveted cotton. He scowled at the bird, then told himself it was the way of all the world, and that birds might as well bear it as men. He had thought he was alone until little Esther's troubled voice startled him. He looked up at the balcony where she stood, a beautiful little vision all in white, with her great sorrowful blue eyes full of tears, watching the distant flutter of wings. He gazed wonderingly up at her until the eyes came back to the nest; then she caught sight of him. She looked at him a moment, perhaps a trifle surprised to find a stranger there, then she said, still with that horror in her voice:

"Did you know there were any such naughty birdies?"

The young man almost laughed, but the little face above him was so grave that he only answered:

"Why, I don't know; why shouldn't there be?"

"But birdies were made to be good and pretty, and sing for God."

He had nothing ready to say to such an astonishing reply as this, but the little maiden went on:

"Poor little birdie! I wish I could do something for her. Now her nest is all torn to pieces."

"You might get her another piece of cotton," he suggested.

She was delighted.

"Could I?" she said, her face all changed in an instant. "Oh! could I? and would she use it?"

"I think she would if you hung it on the branch close to her nest," said he.

"Then I will ask my Grandma for some; and if I come down there will you lift me up, so I can put it on the branch? 'Cause I'm not very tall, you know," she said quaintly.

The little maiden received the promise and vanished through the open window, leaving Robert Knight with the first real smile on his face that had been there in many a day. Presently she came down the wide piazza and stood beside him on the ground.

"Here I am," she said; "and I have some cotton and some silk rav'lings from my dollie's sash—pink and blue. Do you think the birdie would like those, too? My Grandma thought so."

The sweet voice asked his opinion as if it were a matter of great import, and the young man smiled again as he assured her he thought madam-bird would be very glad to get them.

A great time they had arranging them on the branch. Father bird, high up in the branches of the neighboring elm, with his heart in his mouth, watched them, wondering if there was to be an utter destruction of the pretty home he and his wife had labored so hard to make. But perhaps madam-bird saw the pinks and blues and coveted them, for she went and sat very still, beside her husband, looking down, first out of one eye and then out of the other.

The dainty little maiden, mounted on the shoulder of the dark young man, one white arm and hand clasped close about the collar of the dark, rough coat, made a pretty picture, with the maple boughs for a background. They worked eagerly, fixing them "so the birdie would be sure to see them the first thing and not feel bad any more," Esther said; and when it was done they withdrew to the shadow of a large cedar to watch for the return of the householder.

After eying long and anxiously, madam-bird's love for the beautiful overcame her nervous fears, and she came by various short stages, stopping long at each place, to be sure all was well, to the branch where hung the ravelings of dollie's sash. She pecked at them once or twice, turned her head to one side, gave a twittering call to her husband, and down he came. Busy and happy they were then, as any two birds could be, weaving in and out the delicate threads, and making such a nest as would make the heart of Yellow Wings ache with jealousy for many a day.

Oh! how happy was little Esther, down behind the cedar-tree, her small hands clasped together with delight, her eyes very large and bright with excitement. Robert Knight stood near, silently watching her. Presently he remembered that his time was not his own, to stand thus and idle away the hours watching this beautiful little creature. He turned with a scowl and was about to go back to his work, but Esther looked at him with a smile.

"I think you must be a very nice man," she said.

He started. When had any one ever called him nice since his mother used to lay her white hand on his curls and call him her nice boy? It brought a queer sensation in his throat, but he mastered it and said in a rather gruff voice:

"Why?"

"Because you wanted to help the poor birdie so much."

Then she put that soft little hand in his, looked up into his face, and smiled again.

"May I stay with you a little while?" she went on. "What are you doing? I won't bother."

Of course he said "Yes." How could he help it? No one ever said "No" to her when she asked like that.

2

ACROSS the lawn they went together, over to the big flower garden, and Esther sat down on a box of seeds. She was very much interested in the spading of the flower bed, and made him tell her why he did this and that, and what was to be planted in the bed.

"Dowell doesn't dig quick like that. He goes very slow. I think your way is the nicest. Dowell is cross, sometimes, but Grandma says little girls shouldn't bother." Then, after a thoughtful pause, "Do I bother you?"

"Not a bit," he said.

"Then I'll stay a little longer, because I like you," she said.

"You're the only one in the world, then, I guess."

She looked at him in surprise.

"Why, haven't you any Grandma?" she asked pityingly.

He shook his head.

"Nor Grandpa?"

"No."

"And haven't you any mamma?"

Her voice was full of pity now, and it touched him so he could not trust himself to reply, except by another shake of the head.

"Why, then you're just like me, aren't you? I haven't any mamma here, either. She has gone to Heaven. Has your mamma gone to Heaven, too?"

What was this young man, who professed to believe in no such thing as Heaven, to say to this baby's question? He gave a nod which might have meant yes or no, or almost anything else. He couldn't bring himself to say anything against the Heaven which was evidently so real to the little girl. Besides, he felt that, baby though she was, she wouldn't believe him if he should. But Esther took the nod for yes, and went on.

"Was your mamma sorry to leave you all alone, without any Grandpa or Grandma to stay with? My mamma left me with my Grandma and Grandpa. Grandma says she wanted to take me with her, only Jesus had some work for me to do for Him before I went with her, and she said I must do it as quick as ever I could, and come to her, for she would be waiting for me. She said I was to comfort Grandma and Grandpa, and bimeby Jesus would give me something to do for Him, and I must be very good and do it well—just whatever He wanted me to do; then when it was done I could come home to her, where Jesus is, and see Him. Did your mamma leave some work for you to do?"

She paused, her eager blue eyes looking up into his, confidently expecting an answer, and he did not know what to say. His mother's last words came to him and kept him from saying no. He stopped work, with one foot on the top of the spade, and looked at her. How was he going to answer such questions? He could not bring himself to make fun of them.

But the conversation was interrupted just then. A sharp, shrill voice called:

"Esther! Oh, Miss Esther! Where in the world are you? Come right in the house."

"That's my nurse, and I must go. She wants to get me ready for dinner now, but I'm coming out again. You are my new friend, you know, and I like you very much. Good-by."

She was gone, and the young man looked

after her with wonder again. She was such a quaint make-up of womanly dignity and childish innocence. The nurse had come to meet her, and in no very soft tone was admonishing her:

"Miss Esther, what have you been doing down in the garden, talking to that tramp? Don't you know you shouldn't talk to tramps? They're horrid bad men."

His face darkened as he listened, but he could hear the little girl's answer in clear, positive tones:

"Oh no, Sarah! you are mistaken. He isn't a tramp; he is very nice. And besides, his mamma is in Heaven, just like mine, and tramps don't have mammas in Heaven."

Before the little girl had finished speaking there was a softened light in his eyes, and he turned back to his work to hide from himself his unusual excitement.

He wondered often through the day if the little fairy girl would come to speak to him again, but his experience told him she would probably not be allowed to come, and his face grew dark to think that he had sunken so low as to be a gardener, whose only pleasure was to have the little child of the house come and prattle to him. He worked hard, turning up with the rich earth thoughts as hard as the flinty stones he occasionally came across, and it was not until toward evening, just as the sun was throwing his rosy good-night smiles over all the earth, that the little friend of the morning came again.

She stood in her soft white flannel dress, her long gold curls full of the dying sunlight, her little hands clasped behind her, a study in white and burnished gold. He was working still intently, and thinking, hardly noticing that the day at last was done and his work over for a time, until he heard her gentle sigh.

"I came out to say good-night to the sun," she said; "I couldn't come before, because I went to ride with Grandma and Grandpa, but I'm coming out to-morrow if it's a pleasant day. I told my Grandma all about you, and she asked me what your name was, and I had to say I didn't know. Wasn't that funny not to know what a friend's name was? Won't you tell me what your name is?" The queer mixture of woman and baby gleamed from every dimple as she asked this question.

"Robert Knight," he answered. "And what do they call you, little fairy?"

"My name is Esther Carleton. Grandpa calls me his little Queen, but Grandma calls me

God's little servant, because, you know, Queen Esther was a servant when she was a queen. Do you know 'bout Queen Esther?"

"Well, no, I don't know as I do. What about her?"

"Why, you know, she was a queen, an' Hazuerus was a king. He had a friend who hated some of Esther's people and wanted to kill them, and he made the king say they should be killed, and God sent word to Esther to go and ask the king not to kill her people, and it was very hard work, and she was afraid to go, for fear the king would kill her, too, when he found out she was a relation of those people his friend hated; but she went 'cause God told her to, of course, and the king didn't kill her a bit, and he said he would save all those people of hers alive, and so she was God's servant, 'cause she did just what he told her to do. Have you got a story 'bout your name?"

He slowly shook his head: "No, I think not."

But the sinking sun had at last finished his course and slipped away, leaving only a broad band of gold, with a deep crimson thread to mark the place where he had gone out.

"The sun has gone," said little Esther, "and I must go in, for Grandma says the dew begins to fall as soon as the sun gets out of sight. Are you ready to stop now? Hannah says your supper is ready, and my Grandpa says he wants to see you, and I want to-morrow to hurry and come, so I can watch you make garden." She put her soft hand in his, and together they went through the long, dark tree-shadows up the winding gravel path to the house, she chattering, he listening.

The grandfather, careful that the darling of his heart should have no evil companionship, came out and talked long with the young man. By and by he went in and told the white-haired grandmother that he was interested in the young man and had hired him permanently, for Dowell was getting old and lame, and had told him only that morning that he was afraid he would not be able to do all the work that summer. So, at last, Robert Knight had found permanent work.

Nevertheless, in his room over the carriage house, he felt not one whit grateful as he thought it over. The room was large and light and much more comfortable than the one he had been occupying in the miserable boarding-house. The meals to which Hannah called him regularly would be deemed luxurious beside those he had been accustomed to having of late, and he could not deny a certain pleasure when he thought of the strange, beautiful little friend. Still he curled his lip over the work he had "come down to," as he phrased it, and called God hard and unjust—if, indeed, there was a God—which last sentence he never forgot to put in.

The little maiden was on hand bright and early in the morning, sitting on the seed box, a great broad-brimmed hat on the back of her curls, one white satin string in her mouth, and thus she talked eagerly. Queen Esther was always eager.

"Mr. Knight, there is a story 'bout your name. You didn't know it, did you? I was telling my Grandma 'bout you, and how you didn't know any story 'bout your name, and she said that perhaps you were a true knight, and if you were you had a story to work out. Then I asked her what a knight was, and she said it was some one who was sent out to do a brave deed, and she told me a beautiful story 'bout a knight who went out to catch a wicked man and shut him up in prison so he couldn't do any more harm. Are you a knight now, do you suppose?"

The young man felt almost gay that morning, despite the rough clothes and the work that he hated. It was so pleasant to have a companion to talk to him.

"I'll tell you what I'll do, Queen Esther," he said; "queens always have knights, and I'll be your knight if you'll let me."

"My knight!" said Esther. "And what would I have to do? How could you be my knight? What do queens do with knights?"

"Well, I don't exactly know," said he. "You'll have to ask some one else."

"Then I'll ask my Grandma. She knows a great deal. She has a caller now, so I can't ask her yet, but when we have our lunch I'll ask her. Won't that be nice?"

And then the talk drifted into gardening. Little Esther had a great many questions to ask, and wanted to try to spade some for herself. So he held a spade for her, and she put her little white hand into the great round handle, and one small kid shoe on the top of the spade, and pushed and pushed with all her might. Her hat fell off, her face grew very red, and the curls blew into her eyes, but still the stubborn earth would not give way.

"Well, well, well, what are we trying to do now?" came a cheery voice from the shrubbery, and there stood Grandpa, watching and laughing. Esther came down from the spade, her face still very red.

"Oh, Grandpa!" she said, anxiety and disap-

pointment in her face, "I can't do it the way
Mr. Knight does. The spade is too big. When
do you think I'll be big enough to use a spade?
I want to make a garden so much."

"You want to make a garden? What do you
want to do that for? Isn't there garden enough
around here for you?"

"Oh! but, Grandpa, it isn't like having one
all your own, you know, that you made yourself."

"What would you put in your garden if you
had one?"

"Flowers," she said quickly.

"And what would you do with the flowers?" he asked again.

The bright eyes wandered around amongst
the shrubbery as if in search of an answer, but
suddenly they came back to his face, so sweet
and earnest and expectant.

"I would give them to poor sick people
who don't have any at all."

Grandpa looked at her kindly and said:

"Well, little queen, if you want to go to
making garden I'm willing, but you must have
some tools that are not so large and heavy.
Would you like to go into town this afternoon
and get a little hoe and shovel and wheelbarrow?"

Esther's delight knew no bounds. She danced and clapped her hands, she rushed to her grandfather and kissed him again and again.

"You may ask your friend here to show you how, and you shall plant just what you want in your garden," he said indulgently.

So, behold, the next morning Esther came to the garden wheeling before her a little red wheelbarrow, and in it a wee hoe and shovel and rake. Robert Knight had orders to show her how to work in the best way, and to take all the time necessary for it. He began to like his work, with Esther beside him every morning. And more and more the afternoons, when he was alone, would be filled with thoughts of how he could get up some surprise or some new work for the little maiden.

"My Grandma says," she said, one morning, "that kings and queens make people knights and then give them some great work to do. I can't think what to give you to do. Some of the knights were sent after such silly things, but you are my very good knight, so I will have to send you after some great and beautiful thing. Besides, you know, I'm God's little servant, and I must give you something to do that will please Him. We'll think of something nice, Grandma and I, but now you can wait awhile, can't you? You might have to go away from me if I found something for you to do right away, you see, and I don't want you to go away yet. You can wait, can't you? If I'm God's servant He will show me something nice to send you after by and by."

He assured her he would wait as long as she pleased, but it gave him a strange feeling to think he was expected to do something to please God. He didn't believe in God, he told himself, but there was no need to tell this baby so.

3

THE DAYS passed on and the warm lovely summer was at its full. Each day little Esther and her knight, as she so loved to call him, worked in the garden; the flowers blossomed the brightest, the forget-me-nots were the bluest, and the lilies the purest, in the carefully-tended bed in the southwest corner of the garden where the little girl daily worked.

Some ladies, friends of Mrs. Carleton, tried to remonstrate with her. They told her the child would get all rough and brown working so constantly out in the sun, and that they should think she would be afraid to have her with a strange young man, about whom she knew nothing; but Grandma and Grandpa were wise, and were looking out for their darling. The ladies were disappointed in one thing. Esther did not grow brown and rough. Her skin was of that rare, clear kind which would not tan or roughen, and so she only grew rosier and lovelier.

It was a very hot day, and Esther had been left with Sarah while Mr. and Mrs. Carleton went out to dine. She wandered about from window to window, and out on the porch, but everything was uninteresting, and it was so hot everywhere. She wished she were out under that cool maple with Robert. She knew she would have a good time. The house was dull without Grandma, and Sarah was down in the kitchen ironing.

Sarah had told her not to go out of the house until it grew cooler. If Sarah only knew how beautiful it was under that tree she would let her go. She decided to go down to the kitchen and ask her. Down she went, but Sarah was having a discussion with the cook, and did not notice Esther, except to tell her not to lean against the ironing-board or she would be burned. She wandered to the kitchen door. The flowers seemed to be nodding their heads in an afternoon nap, with the trees bending over to fan them. The bees and butterflies went lazily from one flower to another, as though loth to disturb their slumbers. There was a still hum of heat over everything.

She forgot the injunction about the ironing-board and came back to it, leaning one chubby hand and arm, with its short white sleeve, down right in front of the great hissing iron. Sarah had taken her hand from the iron and placed it on her hip, while laboring to convince Bridget, the cook, that Patrick O'Flannigan's sister had run away with a relation of Bridget's own cousin on her mother's side.

Robert Knight was coming down the gravel path outside with the wheelbarrow. Esther heard him and her head was turned toward the door. The ironing-board tipped a little like an inclined plane, as all ironing-boards will when one end is mounted on the table and the other end on a chair-back one inch and a half higher than the table. And so the great hot iron, placed at the upper end while Sarah discoursed on the wickedness of Miss O'Flannigan, came sliding slowly down, hissing and scorching its way as it came, till the soft white arm of little Esther stopped its progress for a moment.

Without a word the little girl jumped quickly, drew back her arm, and the iron proceeded on its wicked way, only stopping at the other end of the board to scorch an ugly spot in Sarah's best white apron ruffle. Little Esther stood looking for a moment at the long red scar in her white flesh, the tears welling up and making her eyes twice as large as usual, her little bosom heaving, and her whole form quivering with pain; then without one sound she turned to the door where stood Robert Knight, and sprang into his arms, burying her head in his neck and letting the deep sobs of pain have full vent, now she had found a refuge and a friend.

Of course they rushed around her to know what was the matter. No one but Knight had seen what had happened. Sarah was fairly frantic, and tried to take her darling from him, but Esther clung to him and he held her fast. It almost seemed as if the burn was his own. He could feel every quiver of pain that went through the little frame as he held her close, and never until then had he realized how she had crept into his heart.

Tenderly they bound up the arm, he holding her the while, for she would not leave him, much to the chagrin of her nurse. When the pain was eased and the little arm all carefully shielded, she felt better and asked him to take her out under the pretty shady trees. So they went out, and he stopped all his work and held her in his arms a long, long time.

When they were fixed to her satisfaction she

leaned back and said, "It hurted very bad, Mr. Knight."

In a tone that almost astonished himself, so full was it of love and revenge for his darling, he said, "How could God let it happen?"

He would have taken the words back the next instant, but they had been in his heart, and had come out before he could stop them. She threw back her head, a startled, wondering look in her eyes.

"Why, Mr. Knight, God didn't let it happen; I did it myself. Sarah told me not to come near the table, and I came. She told me I would get burned, and I did. God sent me word and I didn't mind."

He was startled and ashamed. The little believer's forcible reasoning had silenced him. Her next question startled him yet more.

"Mr. Knight, don't you love my Jesus?"

He couldn't give her any answer but a shake of the head, and he saw she was disappointed.

"Mr. Knight, don't you know my Jesus? He loves you very much."

He shook his head again. The grieved look deepened.

"Then you must find Him right away, for you can't be a good knight unless you know Jesus. How can you go on a great errand unless you know Him? You can't be a brave knight without Him, for you won't have anybody to help you."

She paused, and he looked down at the sad little face, starting to find great tears rolling down her cheeks and dropping thick and fast on his hands. It was anguish to be the cause of those tears. His soul writhed under it. What could he say to comfort her?

"Mr. Knight," came the soft, troubled voice again, "won't you please to go right away and find Jesus? Won't you?"

The pleading eyes, full of tears, looked up at him for an answer, and he felt it was a solemn thing she asked of him, which if he promised he must surely do, and he waited. His proud spirit could not bear to say yes, and he could not say no to his little queen. They heard the distant grind of the carriage wheels as they turned into the gravel driveway, and Esther put up the little well hand and touched him softly on the cheek.

"Won't you please, Mr. Knight?"

"Yes, I will," he said earnestly, and bent over and kissed the bright curl that had strayed out on the breast of his rough coat.

Then Esther was so happy! The tears all melted into smiles, and she wiped her face vigorously with her wee handkerchief, that Grandma might not think her arm "hurted so very much now." The carriage came, and Esther, in the arms of her knight, went to tell Grandma and Grandpa all about the burn. She was carried to the house to be petted, and Grandma was heard to remark that she never would leave her again.

Robert Knight went to his room and set himself to his strange task. To find God! This was solemn business. It was not merely his promise to Esther that had stirred his heart to the depths this afternoon. God's Spirit had been striving with him for some time. The weeks of contact with the lovely life of this trustful little servant of Jesus had softened his heart and set him to thinking. He took up the Bible that had lain untouched on the stand in his room ever since he came there. As he opened it there rushed over him the feeling that he was coming into the presence of the great God, and a sense of his unworthy life filled him with shame. His whole past stood out before him and seemed hateful when he thought that the pure eyes of God were looking upon it. It seemed a hopeless undertaking, this trying to make peace with an angry God, and he felt like giving up all effort; but little

Esther's troubled face came to his mind, and he remembered he had promised.

Back again to his life he went and searched carefully through every detail to see if by any possibility he might find something that would justify him in the eyes of God. He remembered the unkept promise to his dying mother, and fell on his knees beside the chair, crying: "O God, forgive me! I am very wicked. Forgive me and save me, for Jesus' sake!" Over and over again he sent up the same petition, till, worn out by the excitement, he leaned his head against the little table to steady it, and closed his eyes.

There floated through his brain a picture. He saw himself a little boy again, sitting beside his mother in the dim twilight of a Sabbath afternoon, the last faint sunbeam glancing through the stained glass windows of the great dark church, and throwing a glimmer over the white communion-table with its high, stately silver; the sound of a sweet hymn had just died away, and the gentle voice of the white-haired minister was speaking these words:

"Him that cometh to me I will in no wise cast out."

It was a verse his mother had taught him long before, and he remembered the sense of satisfaction which had filled him that afternoon, that the minister had used this verse; but no clear idea of the meaning of those words had entered his mind then. Now he began to realize what they meant. It was a promise from God that He would receive him.

"Him that cometh," he slowly repeated. "Why, I have come already, and He must have received me, for He has promised, but, oh! what shall I do with my wicked, wasted life? It is just filled with sin from beginning to end!"

Then, like an answer to this earnest cry from his awakened soul, came another verse from his childhood memories, and he blessed his mother who had taught him the precious words:

"The blood of Jesus Christ, his Son, cleanseth us from all sin."

Yes, he had known that verse a long time, why had it never brought him such joy as it brought now? But then, he had never before realized what an awful sinner he was. He had often, with his wild companions, sneered at that very verse; at the idea that the blood of Jesus could help any man; but now he felt a blessed relief in the thought that Jesus would bear all the burden of the terrible load he had just begun to see had been upon him for years. With his head still bowed he knelt there a long time, trying to tell Jesus all that was in his heart: the humiliation; the sense of sin; the sorrow; and the overwhelming thankfulness that Christ was willing to save such as he.

"Did you find Him?" whispered Esther in the garden the next morning, while Grandma and Mrs. Senator Brownlee went around amongst the flowers.

"Yes," he answered with a bright smile.

The dreadful burn proved not to be so bad after all, and after a few days the little girl was out among her dear flowers again, very glad to be back and talk to her knight, and glad indeed he was to have her again, for he had missed her sadly.

And then, soon, came Esther's birthday, and she had a party. Nine little girls and ten little boys. They came, their faces shining with the expectation of a good time. How pretty they looked in their dainty dresses and bright sashes flying about among the trees. Madam-bird, just hatching her second brood, sat and watched them, and thought, with a passing bird sigh, how many, many lovely nests all those sashes would make if they were only raveled out. Out under the great elm at the upper end of the lawn, Robert Knight was fixing something about the swing, and around him stood Frankie Elbright, Minnie Haines, Georgie Forbes, and Esther. Little mites they were, with such baby faces, but you should have heard them talk.

"I've got a cousin lives in Boston," said Minnie Haines, with an important little air, "an' she's got a great big doll 's big 's she is, an' it talks, an' walks, an' does ev'ryfing."

"Ho! that's nothin'," said Georgie Forbes. "My papa knows the President," and he swung his little kilts back and forth, and gave a very short jump in the air.

"Presidents ain't as big as kings," said Frankie Elbright. "My papa saw a king once. There ain't anybody bigger'n kings."

Esther had stood very quiet, watching her little guests, but now she said in a positive tone:

"Yes, there is. God is bigger than any one else, and my mamma is in Heaven where she sees him every day, and I'm his little servant."

A queer little hush fell over the baby group, and Georgie Forbes stopped jumping for full half a minute, but Frankie Elbright put his hands in his small pockets, and with the air of some of his elders, walked off saying: "Pooh! That don't count." Robert Knight drew the back of his hand across his eyes before he could see to tie the last knot of the big rope.

But the happy little party was over at last; the summer passed away; Esther's bright flowers sighed and died, except for a few red-mittened geraniums that she helped transplant to the conservatory; and the brilliant autumn came.

4

IT was October. The clear, sharp weather had strewn the lawn and carriage drive with crimson and gold from the boughs of the soft maple-trees, which were scattered so plentifully all about the house. Little Esther, in her long white wool cloak and soft white cap, the gold curls blowing in the breeze, looked like a fair leaf herself, as she stooped to pick the crimson beauties from the gravel. She was gathering a bouquet for Grandma.

How was it that the great iron gates that guarded the carriage drive had been left open that morning! Had Patrick forgotten to close them the night before, or was it that some children had been passing that way and stopped to stand on the iron opener for the fun of seeing the gates slowly swing open, moved by their weight? No one knows. Only the two frantic horses, who fancied they were pursued by the pieces of broken carriage which were attached to them, and which kept hitting their flying heels, saw in that opening a refuge from their enemy, and dashed in. Up the broad drive among the trees, nearer and nearer they came, more maddened by each step, and there was little Esther, stooping down in that gravel drive-way with her back to them, and no one by to watch!

Robert Knight, away at the upper end of the garden, heard their rushing feet, looked up, saw them coming, and saw his little queen just before them. He shouted and ran and made frantic efforts to turn the attention of the furious horses, but he was a long way off and they were close upon his little friend. No one else saw or heard until it was too late. After that nobody seemed to care what other mischief the horses did. Some one caught them—they never knew who—for the servants were all busy rushing here and there after doctors and water and this and that. The doctor came and worked hard and fast for a little time, and by and by the blue eyes opened and looked wonderingly on the group that stood around her.

"Jesus has sent for me. I must go pretty soon.

Where is my knight? Grandma, won't you ask him to come here? I want to tell him something." They made way for him, and he went to her bedside.

"She may live a day or two, and it may be but a few hours," said the doctor to the broken-hearted grandfather. "There are internal injuries. No, she is not in pain—will probably not suffer much."

And so they gathered around their darling for the few short hours that were left to them—the poor grandmother and grandfather and Robert Knight; for Esther wanted her knight with her all the time, and the two old people were ready to grant any request she might make.

"I've found out what to tell you to do, Mr. Knight," she said, with eager voice and shining eyes. "I think an angel whispered it to me just now. I couldn't think of anything beautiful enough to send you to do, but now I know, and it will please Jesus. You must find some people that don't know all about Jesus, and don't know how good He is, and don't love Him, and you must go and tell them all about Him. Will you go, Mr. Knight?"

His voice was too choked to answer, but he bowed his head. The poor grandmother sat close by, sobbing.

"Oh, Grandma!" said the little girl, "please don't cry. I'm going to my mamma and Jesus. You said my mamma wanted me so, only she left me to do some work for Jesus; but now my knight is going to do it for me, and so Jesus has sent for me. Please don't cry, Grandma, dear. You will come so soon, and then we'll all be in Heaven with Jesus."

Now Grandma and Grandpa were getting old, and had been through many sorrows which had at first seemed impossible to bear, but they had found that the Lord had helped them to bear them; and although this was their last little lamb, and dearer to them than life, and to lose her seemed to them harder than anything that had ever come to them before, yet they remembered that Heaven for them was very near, and that the separation could not be for long. So they put their sorrow by and tried to wear bright faces and make the little one's last hours on earth happy ones. They wanted her to feel glad that she was going to Heaven.

"Grandpa," she said, "will you help my knight to do my work for me?"

It was a long, hard afternoon for the three watchers—to feel their darling slipping from them, minute by minute, and not be able to help her; and yet it was a wonderful afternoon. Not one of them would have been willing to lose a moment of it. The little girl was so happy that she was going home to Jesus. She would talk of Heaven, and wonder what it would be like.

"Do you think my mamma will come to meet me?" she asked once. But most of her thoughts were full of her knight and the work he was to do. She charged him many times that he must tell the people how Jesus loved them, and be sure that they all found Him. Then her Grandpa made her very happy by promising that all the money which should have been hers should go to help along the work, and so she planned her pretty angel plans until the sun went down behind the cedar hedge and threw a glory over the room. She had just laid her little hand on Robert Knight's dark, bowed head and said:

"When I get to Heaven I'll go straight to Jesus and tell Him all about my dear knight, and how he is going to do my work for me, and I'll ask Him to help you, and when you get it all done and are ready to come up there too, I'll be at the gate waiting for you, and Grandma and Grandpa will be there too, and my mamma and papa, and your mamma and papa, and Jesus, and we will all be so glad, and the angels will sing"—and the golden head had sunk back upon the pillows. But just as the last glow of sunset lit up the room she raised her head, her face almost gleeful in its brightness, her eyes looking up, her voice very clear:

"I see my Jesus and my mamma; they have come for me. Good-by!"

The bright head sank back upon the pillow and the soft lids closed over the blue eyes. Grandma and Grandpa had no more need to hide their tears, for their darling was beyond "the smiling and the weeping."

Robert Knight went out from that room with the feeling that he had watched the gate of Heaven open and shut again, taking away the dearest thing in life from him; but greater than the deep sorrow which he felt was the solemnity which filled him. He had spent an afternoon in a room where God surely was, waiting to take away one of His own, and he had seen little Esther's face when she had said: "I see my Jesus," and he had felt that she really did. Never again could he be tempted to say there was no God. He knew there was. He had felt His presence. Life was full of a great responsibility that had never been there before. He had been called to a mission, to finish some work for one of Christ's little ones. How he was to do it he did not know, but it was a precious privilege, and he meant to do it. He would begin by telling of Jesus' love to all who came in his way.

He walked out of the front door and down that awful gravel road where only a few short hours before the life and brightness of the house had been, so glad and well; and now she was gone. It was a dreadful thought, but with it also came the remembrance that she was with Jesus, and how glad she had been to go. He shuddered as he crossed the spot where the horses had done their fearful work, and stepped into the grass, just under the maple-tree where madam-bird had first introduced them.

Deep down in the velvety grass, close by the tree trunk, cold and still, its little feet stretched stiffly up to the branches overhead, its bright black eyes glazed over, lay little madam-bird, dead. Poor little bird! He picked her up, with the sad feeling of how Esther would grieve, and instantly came the remembrance that she was where she would never grieve again. As he carried the little bird tenderly out to the garden to bury it in the flower bed she had so loved, he remembered the poem she had learned only a little while before, and recited to him, all about a little sparrow, and how the Heavenly Father knew when one fell to the ground. The blinding tears came thick as he worked, but he knew now that the Heavenly Father cared for him, too.

In the course of the next day he was sent for by Mr. Carleton. He went in, supposing that he was wanted to go on some special errand, but the old man called him into the library and made him sit down. The tears were streaming down his cheeks, his voice was husky and broken, he walked the floor nervously back and forth, his hands behind him, his head bent over. Presently he broke out:

"Knight, we would like to have you take up your education just where you left off. Wife and I have been talking it over and we think it would please the little girl. We would like to have you think it over. It would be the best thing you could do, if you mean to carry out the commission she gave you. It would please her"—

The old man broke down then, but by and by they talked it over more. Robert told him how gratefully he would accept the kind offer, and how much he longed to carry out the wishes of little Esther.

So it came about that only a few days after they had laid the little girl to rest beside her

young mother in the cemetery, Robert
Knight began to prepare for college. He was
growing old to enter college, and it was hard
to go back to study after so long a vacation,
but he worked with a will, remembering his
commission and Esther's words: "I'll ask Him
to help you."

Two people were passing the Carleton
home one day, and one said to the other:
"That little Esther Carleton is dead. Doesn't it
seem a pity that she didn't die when her
mother did? Then the old people wouldn't
have missed her so. It is said that they are very
lonely. I wonder why such little things are
allowed to live at all, if they are not to grow
up. Her life was only long enough to have
those miss her who have had all the care and
trouble of her bringing up."

But what did those two know about it? Her
short bright life was not spent in vain, and
when in Heaven they see her crown they will
understand.

Away out in the Western part of our country, where the people are very poor, and live in
log houses—where they have hard work to
keep soul and body together out of their
scanty farms—stands a little church, neat,
pretty and comfortable. The sun shines on the

white spire, and it reflects a welcome to all the country round, while the bell in the steeple calls many to the house of God. There Robert Knight preaches and teaches, and little Esther's money is helping to bring people to Jesus. Up in Heaven, among the angels, I doubt not she is watching.

And so this little servant's work goes on.

About the Author

Grace Livingston Hill is well known as one of the most prolific writers of romantic fiction. Her personal life was fraught with joys and sorrows not unlike those experienced by many of her fictional heroines.

Born in Wellsville, New York, Grace nearly died during the first hours of life. But her loving parents and friends turned to God in prayer. She survived miraculously; thus her thankful father named her Grace.

Grace was always close to her father, a Presbyterian minister, and her mother, a published writer. It was from them that she learned the art of storytelling. When Grace was twelve, a close aunt surprised her with a hardbound, illustrated copy of one of Grace's stories. This was the beginning of Grace's journey into being a published author.

In 1892 Grace married Fred Hill, a young minister, and they soon had two lovely young daughters. Then came 1901, a difficult year for Grace—the year when, within months of each other, both her father and her husband died. Suddenly Grace had to find a new place to live (her home was owned by the church where her husband had been pastor). It was a struggle for Grace to raise her young daughters alone, but through everything she kept writing. In 1902 she produced *The Angel of His Presence, The Story of a Whim,* and *An Unwilling Guest.* In 1903 her two books *According to the Pattern* and *Because of Stephen* were published.

It wasn't long before Grace was a well-known author, but she wanted to go beyond just entertaining her readers. She soon included the message of God's salvation through Jesus Christ in each of her books. For Grace, the most important thing she did was not write books but share the message of salvation, a message she felt God wanted her to share through the abilities he had given her.

In all, Grace Livingston Hill wrote more than one hundred books, all of which have sold thousands of copies and have touched the

lives of readers around the world with their
message of "enduring love" and the true way
to lasting happiness: a relationship with God
through his Son, Jesus Christ.

In an interview shortly before her death,
Grace's devotion to her Lord still shone clear.
She commented that whatever she had accomplished had been God's doing. She was
only his servant, one who had tried to follow
his teaching in all her thoughts and writing.

Don't miss these Grace Livingston Hill romance novels!

You can find Tyndale books at fine bookstores everywhere. If you are unable to find these titles at your local bookstore, you may write for ordering information to:

Tyndale House Publishers
Tyndale Family Products Dept.
Box 448
Wheaton, IL 60189